The Resurrection Casket

Collect all the exciting new Doctor Who *adventures:*

DOCTOR · WHO

The
Resurrection
Casket

BY JUSTIN RICHARDS

BOOKS

Published by BBC Books, BBC Worldwide Ltd,
Woodlands, 80 Wood Lane, London W12 0TT

First published 2006

ISBN 0 563 48642 2

Commissioning Editor: Stuart Cooper
Creative Director: Justin Richards
Consultant Editor: Helen Raynor
Editor: Stephen Cole
Production Controller: Peter Hunt

Doctor Who is a BBC Wales production for BBC ONE
Executive Producers: Russell T Davies and Julie Gardner
Producer: Phil Collinson

Cover design by Henry Steadman © BBC 2006
Typeset in Albertina by Rocket Editorial, Aylesbury, Bucks
Printed and bound in Germany by GGP Media GmbH, Pößneck

For more information about this and other BBC books,
please visit our website at www.bbcshop.com

For Julian and Chris,
who like pirate stories!

Death was hiding in Kaspar's pocket.

Blurry-eyed, Kaspar slammed down the empty glass. Leaning heavily on the bar, he belched before making his uncertain voyage towards the door of the inn. He knocked against tables, jostled other drinkers, rolling and meandering on his way like a ship skirting the Outreaches. Laughter and abuse rang in his ears in roughly equal measure.

Then he was outside, gulping in the chill night air. It tasted of oil and tar. The sounds of the inn were replaced by the clank and bustle of the port. The creaking of ships and shouting of stevedores. The sign above the door squealed on its hinges as it moved gently in the breeze – swaying back and forth with the same lazy motion as Kaspar as he swayed on his feet. He stared up at it, trying to focus on the cracked, peeling image. It didn't help that the image itself was fractured – a painting of a telescope snapped in half.

The main picture reflected in fragments of painted glass. The Broken Spyglass.

Someone pushed heavily past Kaspar, elbowing him aside. He staggered away, making a tuneless attempt to whistle an old shanty he remembered from his days as a deck swabber on a freight barge on the Jathros run.

As he turned into the alley that ran down the side of the inn, away from the main port, Kaspar realised he was still clutching the few coins Silver Sally had given him as change from his last tankard of grog. He stared at them for a moment, watched them catch the starlight, shining like real gold. Then he closed his hand and thrust his fist into his pocket.

That was when he felt the scrap of paper. Curious, he pulled it out. A folded piece of parchment. Pale and textured in the dim light of the alley. Kaspar grunted, about to drop the paper in the narrow gutter. But he didn't. Some spark of curiosity at the back of his woozy mind made him pause to open it.

And suddenly he was sober. Suddenly he was seeing clearly. Staring at the mark on the paper – a simple black shape. A smudge of ink. A vague form that meant nothing. Except to an old pirate. And Kaspar had done his time on a rusting galleon at the edge of the Gerossic Rift. He had seen the shape before, knew it instantly. Understood what it meant.

The Black Shadow.

Someone had put the Black Shadow on him.

Like a curse. A threat. Sentence of death.

Getting rid of it would do no good now, so he jammed the paper back in his pocket. Already he was running. Already he was heading back towards the light, towards people and safety. Though he knew that, really, nowhere was safe. Already he could hear the thump of feet on the cobbles behind him. He could imagine the glint of the knife in the starlight. He could feel the hot breath of the killer on the back of his neck.

His own heart thumped. His eyes watered, blurring everything. His breath rasped. He tried to tell himself it was all imagination. There was no one there. The alley had been empty. The paper – it was a joke, or a mistake. Or just a smudge of ink on a receipt from the Spyglass...

Except that suddenly it was real. A dark shape was materialising out of the air in front of Kaspar. A huge, shaggy form turning towards him. As if the night had somehow coalesced into a massive version of the blotted shape on the parchment.

Kaspar stumbled to a halt, turned, started to run the other way. Felt the heavy hand on his shoulder as it dragged him back, turned him again. Only it wasn't a hand. It was a paw, covered in dark hair with fingers that ended in sharp claws. Eyes burned red out of the blackness high above him. Hot, rancid breath scalded the air and made him cough.

And a deep voice that grated like the broken glass on the inn sign said, 'Look, I'm really sorry about this.'

Claws glinted like knives as they caught the starlight.

'Really, *really* sorry. No, I mean it.'

Raked down at Kaspar's screaming face.

'But, well, you know how it is.'

Kaspar knew nothing except blackness. A body slammed to the ground. Blood ran in the gutter, washing a slip of folded paper away with it. And the smudge of darkness shook its head sadly and was gone...

The only constant light was shining up from beneath the floor plates. A pale yellow glow that tinged the air like faint mist and made the Doctor's face look shadowed and angular as the main lights flickered and flashed apparently at random.

'So what's going on?' Rose asked.

'Going on? It's all going completely mad. Every sprocket and wocket and mergin-nut. Mad, mad, mad.' He slammed a lever across as if to show how it made no sense at all.

The light was fading, the Doctor's face getting darker. Then, abruptly, it glared into brilliance, making both the Doctor and Rose screw up their eyes.

'Time for a service?' Rose suggested. She wasn't worried. Not really. Not yet. Whatever the problem was, the Doctor would fix it soon enough. Probably. 'Should have got a ten-million-mile service back on New Earth.'

'I dunno, you materialise for a split second in real

space-time to take a bearing and see what happens?'
The Doctor was shaking his head, clicking his tongue,
moving quickly round the console. 'What's the
scanner say?'

Rose glanced at the screen. 'Sort of whirly stuff.'

The Doctor paused, hand over a control. 'Whirly
stuff? That could be bad. How much whirly stuff? I
mean, a few whirls or the inside of a clock?'

'You know that screensaver Mickey has on his
computer with pipes that keep growing till they fill the
screen?'

He sucked in a deep breath. 'Well, that's not good.
Here, let's have a look.' The Doctor was leaning over
Rose's shoulder, his fingers tapping out a rhythm she
could feel through her jacket.

'Problem?'

He nodded. 'EMP signature. Electromagnetic pulse.
Like you get in a nuclear… whatsit.' He waved his
hands to demonstrate. 'Whoosh. You know.'

'I know. Cities getting cooked.'

'Sort of thing,' he agreed. 'Only it just goes on and
on. Look at it. Whirly stuff. Like there's a thousand
bombs going off one after another. With no let-up.
Must be hell out there.'

'Then let's stay in here,' Rose suggested. 'Where it's
safe.'

'Ah.'

'It is safe?' She peered at him through the flickering
light. 'Tell me it's safe.'

'Er.'

Then the console exploded.

'Stay exactly where you are, all right?'

'Er, why?'

'Wiring's gone a bit crazy. Anything could be live, anything could go wrong, anything could explode or collapse or… something.'

'Something bad I'm guessing, right?' Rose sighed. 'OK, not going anywhere,' she said, and was surprised that her voice was shaking. The light was strobing and flashing like a demented disco. 'Can't we stop the lights doing that?'

'Working on it. Not a problem. All under control.' His voice broke off with a cry of pain. The Doctor's face was suddenly white in a flash of sparks. 'Right,' he went on after a moment, 'that'll be the live one then. Nearly there now.'

Rose waited as the lights continued to flash and flicker.

'OK, lied about that, sorry,' the Doctor said. He was sucking his fingers. 'Not even close. The whole thing's gone barmy. That's a technical term, by the way. Barmy – means, well, barmy really. Tell you what…' His head ducked down behind the console and there was a scraping sound – a drawer opening perhaps? Then a rasping Rose recognised as the tear of a match head across the rough side of the box. A tiny flare of light as the Doctor stood up again, holding a match. 'Got it!'

'A match? All right, a whole box of matches. That's

not very high-tech.'

'Works, though. No moving parts, no electrical circuits to be affected by the EMP. In case the lights go out and so I can see to work properly without the flickery do-dahs.'

'Right. So how long's that match going to last?'

'For ever.' He picked his way carefully across to her like he was dancing over stepping stones and held the match up close to her face so she could get a good look at it.

'What?'

'Everlasting match. Look – not burning down.'

'That's impossible.'

He grinned at her through the flame. 'Can't have had breakfast yet, then. It's made of Umbeka wood. From the Umbeka trees that grow on the planet...' He sucked in his cheeks as he tried to remember. 'The planet... The planet Umbeka. It has a long, cold, wet winter, lasts for centuries. But the summer's only a couple of weeks.'

'Sounds like England.'

'Much the same. Only the summer, when it does come, is hot. *Really* hot. The heat stimulates the wood and it grows.'

She understood now. 'So the wood of the match is still growing?'

'Yeah, stimulated by the heat of the flames, it grows at just the same rate as it's consumed by the fire. Neat, huh?'

'Yeah. Neat.'

'Good system. Just what you need on a planet with a long winter – everlasting firewood. Ecologically pretty sound too.'

'Just one question,' Rose told him.

'Anything – ask me anything. I'm an Umbeka expert. Got top grade in Umbeka, me.'

'How's it help us get the TARDIS working properly again?'

'Ah.'

'Ah,' she echoed.

'Er.'

'Er? Is "er" good? Doesn't sound good.'

'Well, no, not completely good. Good-ish. We either need to wait for the EMP to stop, which it doesn't seem is going to happen any time soon. Or we need to move the TARDIS out of its influence.'

'And how do we do that?'

'Oh, loads of possibilities there. Spaceship, lorry, fork-lift truck. Maybe a team of highly trained squirrels. We'd need a lot of them, mind.'

Rose was watching the match as it didn't burn down. 'Doesn't that mean going outside?'

'Mmm.'

'Through the doors that aren't opening because all the controls are knackered?'

'Mmm. Another technical term there, like it.'

'Into a nuclear… whatsit.'

The Doctor's head bobbed about as he considered

this, then settled into a nodding motion. 'Exciting, isn't it? I'd better find some anti-radiation pills. Wonder where I put those. Under A for Anti-radiation maybe. Or R for Radiation.' He clicked his tongue loudly and rapidly before hurrying back to the console across the imaginary stepping stones.

'Could be P for Pills,' Rose suggested.

'T for Tablets,' he countered.

'W for Whatsit.'

He sighed. 'Blast.'

'Yeah, could be under B,' Rose agreed.

'No, I meant *blast*. As in, they could be anywhere.' He pulled open a little drawer on the console, apparently at random. 'Yep – here they are.' He took out what looked suspiciously like a plastic box of Tic Tac mints. 'Right, next it's D for doors,' he decided as he passed her a small pale pill. 'Since the door control now seems to turn the scanner on and off. Or possibly it's C for Crank.'

There was a crank handle in a cupboard close to the main doors. Rose watched with a mixture of amusement and apprehension as the Doctor fitted it into a small socket under the telephone and began to turn. She was holding the match so he could see what he was doing as the lights continued to flicker and fade and flash around them. The pill the Doctor had given her was bitter and chewy – like a small, lemon-flavoured fruit gum. It seemed to take for ever to get rid of it – everlasting tablet, maybe. The doors creaked and groaned as he turned the handle.

'So what else can cause this EMP thing, apart from a nuclear explosion?'

'Oh, lots of things. Like, you know…' He continued to turn the handle and the doors juddered and began to move. 'Could be… well, anything really. Like I said. Lots of things.'

'Give me a for-instance.'

'What, off the top of my head?'

'Off anywhere you like.'

There was a gap between the doors now. Outside looked dark, but not as dark as in the TARDIS.

The Doctor paused to get his breath back. 'Can you get through there?' he asked, meaning the narrow gap between the doors.

'Only in my dreams,' Rose told him.

'I probably can,' he said. 'Only teasing.' He set back to work. 'Outside,' he went on, more seriously, 'is probably a wasteland. Be prepared for that. Aftermath of a war on this scale isn't much fun. People suffering dreadfully, if they've even survived. Death, destruction, devastation. Lots of "D" words really. Bit of a disaster.'

The gap was wide enough now and Rose squeezed through. She stood just outside the door and stared at the scene in front of her. It was night, stars shining brightly above her, and the scene illuminated by what looked like gas lamps. She blew out the match.

'I can see something,' Rose said loudly, 'that doesn't begin with D.'

'What?'

'I think it's a pub.' She gingerly touched the business end of the Doctor's everlasting match. It was cool, so she pushed it into her jacket pocket.

A shadowy figure was heading their way. The TARDIS was in a narrow street with high brick walls on either side. There was just about room for the figure to get past.

There was a lamp on a bracket high on the wall and, as the man stepped under it, Rose expected to see signs of the terrible mutilation or burns from the explosion. The man hesitated, looked up, and stared straight at Rose. His face was weathered and old, his beard grey and matted, and what hair he had left was in tufts round the edge of his balding head.

'Good grog, that,' he rasped. 'Do a good pint in the Spyglass, they do.' Then he gave her a short wave and carried on down the street.

'Well, I didn't expect this,' came the Doctor's enthusiastic voice from beside her. 'Pleasant surprise, isn't it?' Rose watched as the Doctor's grin slowly changed to a puzzled frown. 'So I wonder what's up with the TARDIS,' he said.

ONE

Rose was saved from having to answer the Doctor by the click of the TARDIS's doors closing behind him.

'Safety measure,' the Doctor said sadly. 'Keeps the interior in stasis till she gets back to normal.'

'So they close themselves till you open them again?' That seemed sensible.

'Yes, well. Not quite.' The Doctor peered into the distance, avoiding Rose's gaze. 'Absolutely correct, right up to the bit about opening them again.' His voice was fading as he walked briskly away and Rose ran to catch up with him – in time to hear him say, 'Once the doors are shut, they stay shut.'

'Stay shut? What, for ever, like the match?'

'No. That would be daft. Just till she can repair her systems and get everything working properly again.'

'And let me guess, we can't open them with that starting-handle thing either. Because that would be daft.'

'No, completely wrong. We can't open them with the starting-handle thing because it's still inside.'

'And so the plan is, what exactly?'

They were at the end of the alley, looking out across a busy courtyard that was much better lit than the alley. People were hurrying back and forth, carrying crates and boxes, pushing small trolleys, shouting and cursing.

'Market?' the Doctor wondered. 'Plan is to find out what's emitting the constant pulses, and stop it. Then the TARDIS will sort itself out and we'll be on our way. Easy.'

'Easy,' Rose echoed. 'And s'pose we can't? S'pose it's something important that we can't turn off?'

'Can't be anything too important. I mean, look – level-two stuff at most here. Low technology, pre-electricity.' His eyes narrowed and he nodded slowly. 'I think this is a port. Probably, what, eighteenth century. Might be Bristol.'

'Did they have steam power in the eighteenth century?' Rose asked.

'Just about. Pretty rudimentary but they were getting there. Why?'

Rose just pointed. Across the square, the crowds of people were parting to make way for something. Rose had heard it before she saw it – puffing and blowing, wheels rattling over the cobbles. Then the clouds of white steam. Finally the vehicle appeared through its own mist – metal, squat, functional and bland. It was just a large barrel of a boiler on heavy metal wheels, with huge pistons angled down between the body and the axles. It was pulling a long trailer loaded with crates.

'That is just a bit more sophisticated than I'd have expected,' the Doctor conceded. 'Let's see where it's going.'

The vehicle was turning in a wide arc which brought it quite close to where the Doctor and Rose were standing. As it passed, they were enveloped in warm, oily steam. The steam cleared, leaving the Doctor standing alone, looking round in confusion.

'Rose?' he shouted.

She waved to him from where she was perched on the back of the low trailer. 'Come on! Who knows how far this thing's going? I'm not traipsing miles through the night after it. Might be going to Carlisle.'

They sat side by side, swinging their legs. Rose watched the people as they passed them. The Doctor was right, the place seemed like a busy seaport. Maybe they were headed for the docks to load a ship.

The Doctor was leaning back against a crate and looking up at the sky. 'I don't think we're going to Carlisle,' he said at last.

'York?' Rose suggested.

He shook his head. 'Stars are wrong. And there's no moon.' He sat up straight again. 'This isn't Earth.'

'You're kidding.'

As she spoke, the trailer drew alongside a wall and

stopped. Except it wasn't a wall. It was a vertical sheet of riveted metal. It stretched high above Rose and the Doctor. She looked up – and up – until she could make out the shape of the entire ship.

'OK, so you're not kidding,' Rose admitted. 'Wonder where we are, then. And when.'

It was certainly a ship. Smoke was rising lazily from several funnels; masts and rigging projected from the hull. But it was all at a crazy angle – as if someone had stood a steamship on its back end. And at the bottom, below the level of the quay where Rose and the Doctor were climbing off the trailer, they could see massive exhaust nozzles.

'Top half a mix of steam and sailing ship,' Rose said. 'Bottom half, space shuttle. Does that mean what I think it does?'

The Doctor's answer was drowned out by the noise. It came from further along the quay, where Rose could now see there were more of the strange metal vessels moored. One of them was shaking, steam erupting suddenly from beneath it. The masts slowly folded downwards until they were flat against the side of the metal deck.

'Amazing,' the Doctor shouted above the building rush and roar of the steam. 'To get that much thrust…' He whistled in appreciation.

And the massive metal steamship roared even louder as it lifted slowly and majestically into the night. White clouds blew across the Doctor and Rose, making everything warm and foggy. When they cleared, Rose could see the ship disappearing into the sky, the red glow of its furnaces fading into the distance.

'Why steam?' she wondered out loud. 'Why not something more... modern?'

The Doctor did not reply. He was still staring after the ship, tapping a finger against his lips.

'Because of this pulse thing, isn't it?' she realised. 'No technology works, so they have to use old-fashioned methods like steam and stuff.'

'Seems likely.'

'But that means we can't just shut it off, whatever it is.'

'Seems likely.'

'I mean, it could be a natural phenomenon, something in the atmosphere or whatever.'

'Seems likely.'

'That's not helping.'

'More than likely.'

'So what now?'

He shrugged. 'Dunno really. I think we're probably stuffed.'

'Oh, Mr Optimism. Great.'

He grinned, but Rose could see the anxiety still in his eyes. 'We're going to need help. Need to know what's going on. Then we can revise our plan.'

'Tourist Information Centre?' Rose asked. 'If in doubt, ask a policeman?'

'If in doubt,' the Doctor corrected her, 'ask at the pub.'

The sky was lightening as they reached the Broken Spyglass. A pale orange glow tinged the air, though Rose could still see the stars shining through it. A pinprick of white light moved slowly among the tiny dots and Rose wondered if it was the ship they had seen blasting off or another.

On the way they had passed several more of the steam-powered carts, and also a bulky, oily steam-driven approximation of a man. Puffs of white smoke erupted from the primitive robot's joints as it moved. Its face was like an old tin toy Rose had seen at a car boot sale, only stained with oil and crusted with rust. It hurried past them, wheezing its way towards the quay and whatever business it had there.

'So this whole place runs on kettle power?' she said as the Doctor pushed the door of the inn open.

'Seems likely.'

'Don't start that again.'

'Sorry.'

There were wall lamps burning, and candles on the tables. They had burned down low during the night but now the grubby windows were glowing orange with the light from outside. It looked like an old-fashioned, olde-worlde pub, Rose thought. The walls were panelled with dark, stained wood. Plain wooden tables stood on a bare stone-flagged floor. Uneven stone floor, she thought as she caught her toe on the edge of one of the slabs. At the end of the room was a long wooden bar complete with hand pumps, and a flight of stairs led to a gallery above.

There were few people in the inn. A couple of bleary-eyed men were playing something that looked like dominoes, but with stars rather than dots on the playing pieces. They glanced up at the Doctor, stared a bit longer at Rose, then went back to their game. At another table, an older man sat alone, staring at his near-empty glass. A near-empty bottle stood beside it.

Rose thought that was it, apart from the girl behind the bar. She looked about the same age as Rose, with short dark hair. She was talking to someone at the side of the room, standing sideways so that Rose could only see her profile. Faint mist was curling up through the air around her, maybe smoke from a cigarette or steam from hot water in a basin below the bar...

'Don't be soft, Jimm,' the girl was saying loudly. 'It's not Bobb. He'll still be asleep. He won't have missed you yet.'

But when Rose looked across at the table the girl was addressing, there was no one there. Or rather, the person at the table had ducked down behind it when the Doctor and Rose came in. Now he peered timidly over the top, deep brown eyes staring out from under a mess of black hair. When he pulled himself back into his chair, still watching Rose warily, she could see he was a boy of about ten. She smiled at him, and the boy looked quickly away.

'I think we scared him,' the Doctor said quietly. 'Can't have that, can we?' And he wandered cheerily over and sat down opposite the boy. 'Hi there,' he said. 'I'm the Doctor and this is Rose. People don't usually hide behind the furniture from us. Can I get you a lemonade or something? What'll you have, Rose?'

Rose smiled at the boy – Jimm, the girl had called him – and turned to the bar to see if she could spot a bottle of something that didn't look too dangerous. Her smile froze as the girl turned to face her and Rose could see where the mist was coming from.

The girl was only half there.

One of the shoulders that emerged from the top of her blouse was metal – riveted and jointed. Rose guessed the whole of her left arm was also mechanical, as it ended in a metal gauntlet-like hand at the end of the sleeve. Tiny rods and pistons traced the fingers and the shoulder joint was a greasy ball-and-socket connection. Puffs of steam blew out when the girl moved her arm, and every movement was accompanied by a faint hiss of changing pressure. Like the robot they had passed – steam technology, but more sophisticated and streamlined.

The most striking thing was the girl's face. Again, it was only half there. Curved, tarnished metal plates replaced one cheek and a bronze plate covered the left eye. The skin was dark and discoloured where it met the metal. The right side of the girl's face was attractive and smiling. The left was unforgiving metal, hissing and spitting steam as she moved. Only the mouth ran the whole width unbroken, but metal lips encased one side. Rose swallowed and tried to reinstate her smile.

'That's Silver Sally,' the boy said. 'She's my friend.'

'Hi,' Rose said in a hoarse whisper.

'Have a drink with us?' the Doctor asked. 'I'm assuming…' His voice trailed off and he gave an embarrassed shrug.

But the girl laughed. 'Oh, I can down a pint of grog as well as you can,' she said. 'And I need water too – to top up the reservoir that feeds the steam pistons.'

'Of course. The Doctor's grin was restored. 'Well, whatever. I'll have a pint of grog, and Jimm here can have the same again, and Rose?'

'Water,' she decided. 'Just water.'

'Just water,' Silver Sally echoed.

'In a dirty glass,' the Doctor told her quickly.

The glass was actually a pewter tankard and it seemed clean enough. The water was cold and wet and tasteless. Jimm was drinking something that looked yellow, and the Doctor gulped appreciatively at his grog, which he said reminded him of something called 'Old Codger'. Rose thought she'd stick with the water.

Sally was turning down the lamps and clearing away the candles as the light improved, and Jimm was telling them he'd have to be off home soon. 'My uncle doesn't like me coming here.'

'That'd be Bobb,' the Doctor said, delighted. 'So, Bobb's your uncle!'

'Yes, he is,' Jimm told him, evidently puzzled at the Doctor's amusement.

'You are a bit young to be down the pub,' Rose pointed out.

'I don't mean just here,' Jimm replied. 'He doesn't like me being near the docks, near the ships.'

'So why come?' she asked. 'Is it to see Sally?'

'Well, yeah. I suppose. But the ships too.' His eyes glinted in the orange light as he leaned across the table, suddenly animated and excited. 'Seeing them taking off. The smell, the heat of the steam. Just the sight of it! I love it, everything about it. I'm going into space one day,' he told them with determination. 'I don't care what Uncle Bobb says about the danger and the sort of people who work on the steam freighters and at the docks. I'm gonna do it. You watch me.'

'If we're here, we certainly will,' the Doctor assured him. 'But you need to wait a bit yet, I think.'

'Yeah, if you're that keen your uncle will understand,' Rose said.

Jimm grunted, unconvinced, and went back to his yellow drink.

'So,' the Doctor said brightly, 'what happened to Sally, then?'

Rose kicked him under the table, and he gave her a pained 'What?' expression.

'Yeah,' Rose said quickly, 'how come technology and

electricity and everything don't work here, then?'

Jimm frowned at them. 'Because of the zeg.'

'Zeg?'

'We're new here,' the Doctor explained. 'Just passing through. Doing an assessment for the Intergalactic Tourist Bureau. See?' He held out a leather wallet opened to show an official-looking badge. Rose knew that the badge wasn't really there at all – it was a blank sheet of slightly psychic paper tuned so that it showed people whatever the Doctor wanted them to see.

'Tourists won't want to come here,' Sally said, plonking down another three drinks with a hiss and a blur of steam. She collected a tankard from the bar and sat down at the table with them.

'Why's that, then?' the Doctor asked.

'Like Jimm says. Cos of the zeg. It's a zone of electromagnetic gravitation. Interferes with anything that has an electrical circuit. Why I'm stuck in the steam age,' she added, sticking her arm out by way of demonstration. It was wreathed in warm, damp mist that settled slowly as condensation on the wooden table top.

'Like an EMP,' the Doctor said, pleased with himself. 'Only constant.'

'Something like that. Can't say I understand it. But it covers the whole system, as far as the Outreaches. You need a steamship any closer in than that.'

'Lots of ships get stranded in the Outreaches,' Jimm said. 'Used to happen all the time in the old days, before they knew about the zeg and understood what was going on. Even now, some ships get it wrong. They drift off course and get stuck. Everything shuts down or goes haywire and they're stranded.'

'So why do people come here at all?' Rose wondered. 'Aside from the drinks?'

'It's a living,' Sally told her. 'This is the last working port, the last civilisation where you can refuel and take on supplies, before the mining belt.'

'But if that mining belt is inside this zeg thing, why don't they just mine somewhere else?' the Doctor asked. 'There must be loads of other places to go. But here, with no technology to speak of, they'd have to do it all by hand.' He waved his arms about by way of demonstration in case anyone had missed the point. 'Pick and shovel, axe and spade, hammer and tongs.'

'That's what some of them like. The pioneering spirit. Old frontier, new worlds. Sort of thing.'

'And the belt's so rich in trisilicate and stooku,' Jimm said, 'you can make your fortune.'

'I bet,' Rose said.

Sally laughed, the real side of her face creasing into a smile while the metal side remained placid and unchanged. 'You're right, it doesn't happen often.'

'Everyone thinks they'll find a stooku seam,' Jimm said excitedly. 'Or a new mineral like falastid, or even Hamlek Glint's lost treasure.'

'Hamlek Glint's lost treasure?' the Doctor asked.

'Where did he lose it?' Rose said.

'No one knows,' Jimm said, confused. 'That's why it's lost.'

'It's just a story,' Sally said abruptly. 'Even if Glint existed, I don't think his treasure did.'

'It did!' Jimm insisted. 'I know it did.'

'So do I,' said another voice.

Rose hadn't realised how loud they were getting. Now the old guy at the next table was calling across to them.

'You and your fake artefacts,' Sally said.

'They're real, I'll have you know,' the old man insisted.

'Yeah, and so's my arm.' She waved it in a swirl of steam to make her point.

'They're real,' the man said again. 'Got a good price for the last one, we did. From Drel McCavity, no less.'

'Drel McCavity?' the Doctor said. 'He the local dentist?'

'He owns all of this planet – the whole of Starfall,' Jimm said. 'Gets a commission on every sale, takes a fee for every mooring. And he collects anything to do with Hamlek Glint, like my uncle.'

'What, *anything*?' The Doctor's eyes narrowed as he wondered about this.

'Artefacts. Papers. Anything.'

Sally was still talking to the man. 'You're crazy, Rodd,' she was telling him. 'OK, so the stuff's the right period, but there's no proof it ever belonged to Glint, no proof it was part of his takings. And you'd do well to realise that before you go the same way as poor old Kaspar.'

The man stared at her for a while, then lapsed again into silence.

'Sorry,' Sally said. Half her face looked embarrassed. 'Kaspar died last night,' she explained quietly. 'They found him in the alley outside.'

'So how do you know his stuff's not real?' Rose asked in a whisper.

'Jimm told me.'

That surprised Rose, and she looked at Jimm, who shrugged.

'My uncle has the biggest collection of Glint – bigger than McCavity's even. He wouldn't buy it, said it wasn't genuine.'

'But apparently this McCavity had a different opinion,' the Doctor said.

The man, Rodd, stood up, his chair falling over backwards as it caught on the uneven floor. He pulled a handful of coins and a few notes from his pocket and put them down on the table.

Sally stood up. 'No offence.'

'None taken,' he said gruffly, pushing a few coins and a note across the table and collecting up the rest to put back in his pocket. Then he paused, hand hovering over a piece of paper. Rose could see that it wasn't a banknote – it was plain white, whereas the notes were pale green. Slowly Rodd picked up the paper and unfolded it. His eyes widened in surprise. Surprise turned to horror. He swallowed hard and, still staring at the paper, turned and stumbled from the inn.

The door slammed shut behind him.

'What's up with him?' Rose said.

'He's been drinking all night,' Sally said. 'Not surprised really, after his friend was killed. Thick as thieves, they were – and I mean that pretty literally in their case. Him and Kaspar, and Edd and Bonny.'

'This Kaspar?' the Doctor asked. 'So, what happened?'

'Dunno. They think it was some wild animal.'

'Maybe a wolfling, got in from the wastelands,' Jimm said. His face was pale. 'They say his body was ripped all to pieces.'

There wasn't another ship due to leave that morning, so the docks were quiet. The night shift had gone and the morning shift was not in any rush to take over. Rodd found himself walking hurriedly along the deserted West Quay.

His quickest way home was down the alley at the side of the pub. But that was where Kaspar's body had been found. Rodd wasn't superstitious, but neither was he one to tempt fate. He took the long route, breathing in the oily, steamy air by the berthing bays. Most of them were empty, and the last contained only a steam clipper being refitted for a run to the Maginot Station.

He could see a sailor sitting on the low wall at the

end of the bays, silhouetted against the rising suns. Rodd could imagine the man lighting a pipe, staring into the sky and thinking of past journeys and his next voyage. It was years since Rodd had worked the clippers, but he still felt a pang of nostalgia. Life had seemed much simpler then…

As he approached, he prepared to call out to the sailor. To say hello. But there was something odd about the figure that was turning slowly towards him. Rodd could make out the details of the wall now – the stonework and mortar. But the figure was still a dark silhouette. And it was far larger than Rodd had thought. Massive, in fact. A giant.

A monster.

The huge, dark, hairy creature jumped down from the wall and walked over to where Rodd was standing frozen to the spot with fear. It took long, lazy strides, large paws hanging down by its side like an ape. Rodd thought he could hear the clip of its claws as they clicked against the cobbles. But then he realised it was the chattering of his own teeth. In his mind he turned to run, but his body didn't move.

The creature's head was tilted to one side as it regarded Rodd through blood red eyes. Large fangs dripped saliva as it opened its mouth to speak.

'Like I told your friend,' the monster said, 'I'm really sorry about this. But, you know, a job's a job.'

It paused, as if to hear what Rodd thought about this. But Rodd was unable to answer. His mouth was moving but all that came out was a high-pitched, anguished whine.

The creature sighed, its massive chest heaving. 'Still, a nasty murdering monster's gotta do what a nasty murdering monster's gotta do.' It stepped closer, blotting out the suns with utter hairy blackness. 'Sorry, mate.'

'You got somewhere to stay?' Sally asked, on her way to deliver drinks to dockers just in from the night shift.

'Did have,' Rose said. 'But we got locked out.'

'We've got rooms here. Could do with some company,' she said on her way back.

'You own this place?' the Doctor asked.

'Get real!'

'McCavity owns all the land, takes rent,' Jimm told them. 'He's making a killing.'

'Bit of a despot, is he?' the Doctor wondered.

'A what?'

'Tyrant,' Rose translated.

'What, like Glint? No, he's all right. Lets people get on with their lives. Starfall's OK. But I'll be glad to get away,' Jimm admitted.

'You leaving?' Rose said.

'Soon as I can find a ship that'll let me work my passage.'

'Might be a while, then,' the Doctor said with a smile.

Jimm smiled sadly back. But his smile turned rapidly into a look of frightened despair as the inn door flew open and a man stepped inside. He was a big man, broad-shouldered and tall, though he walked with a stoop as he advanced menacingly on the Doctor, Rose and Jimm. His face was weathered and lined, grey stubble clinging to his chin and straggly white hair thinning across his head.

'I thought I'd find you here, lad,' he growled as he reached the table.

Jimm was pale and leaned back in his chair, as if trying to keep well away from the man. 'I've not been here long, Uncle Bobb. Really, I haven't.'

Uncle Bobb grunted. 'Half the night I expect by the look of you.' He glanced at Rose, then the Doctor. The Doctor grinned back. 'These friends of yours?'

'Rose, and the Doctor,' Jimm explained.

'Hi,' the Doctor said. He reached out over the table to shake hands, but Bobb took hold of his hand and examined it.

'You don't work in the docks or on the ships.'

'No. True. Got me there.'

'In fact, I doubt if you work at all.' He paused to look at Rose. 'Either of you.' Then he turned his attention back to Jimm. 'Go on, then – go and tell Sally to put it all on my tab.' He waited till Jimm had scurried nervously off to the bar to talk quietly to Silver Sally, then leaned across the table and addressed the Doctor: 'I hope you've not been filling the lad's head with space stories and tales of pirates.'

'Of course not,' the Doctor assured him. 'I expect he gets enough of that at home, doesn't he? He was telling us about Hamlek Glint. Who was he – a privateer?'

Bobb's face cracked into a half-smile. 'You don't know about Glint?'

'No,' Rose said. 'But we're told you're the man to ask.'

'Probably true. But right now I need to sort out that young lad. Space isn't all swashbuckling and treasure and he needs to know that.' He turned to Jimm. 'Once you've got a decent breakfast inside you, then you've got some sorting and cataloguing to do.' He turned back to Rose and the Doctor, telling them, 'That'll teach him there's more about sailing through space than he thinks. Once he's measured and sketched and recorded a few sextants and astro-rectifiers and levelometers.'

Jimm was back, head hanging and kicking his feet. 'Sorry, Uncle Bobb,' he muttered.

The old man ruffled the boy's hair affectionately. 'That's all right. I know what it's like when you get the space bug. But you stay at home, don't wander off.' He turned back to the Doctor and Rose. 'Thanks for looking after him. If you have time later, come round and hear about Hamlek Glint – Scourge of the Spaceways.'

'Oh, can they?' Jimm said in delight. 'Can I show them the collection, can I?'

'We'll see.' Bobb was smiling now. 'Good day to you,' he said to the Doctor and Rose. 'Sally can tell you where to find us.' He took his nephew's hand and led him to the door.

Jimm turned and waved, then the door closed and they were gone.

'What a nice man,' the Doctor said. He sounded surprised and impressed. 'If only everyone was as nice as that, the universe would be so... *nice*.'

'So what's the plan now?' Rose asked.

'We just need to get the TARDIS out of this zeg whatsit, then we're all hunky-dory.'

'And how do we do that?'

'Sally?' the Doctor called. 'What's the chance we can charter a ship, or buy space in a freighter?'

'To where?' she called back. 'Maginot?' She was talking to a young man and a girl – come to take over manning the bar, Rose imagined.

'Anywhere out of the zeg,' the Doctor said.

She considered, the real side of her mouth turning slightly downwards. 'You got tons of cash?'

'No,' the Doctor admitted happily. 'Not a bean.'

'Lucky Bobb bought your drinks then or you'd be washing up for a week. We'll talk about how you want to pay for your room later.'

'Rooms, plural,' Rose pointed out. 'So what's the chance of begging board and lodgings on a ship?'

Sally laughed, steam hissing round her as she moved. 'No chance at all.' She thought for a moment, then added, 'There's a clipper being refitted at the end of the quay. It's heading for Maginot. They might let you crew for them, if they're not already fully manned.'

'We've got this big blue box,' Rose told her. 'We need to take it with us.'

Sally laughed again. 'Tell them that *after* they say they'll take you.'

The clipper wasn't hard to find – it was the last ship berthed on the quay that Silver Sally had directed them to. It was far smaller than the enormous steamship that Rose and the Doctor had watched take off earlier. More like a large yacht, but again it was up-ended, and the mid-section included a vast metal drum that Rose guessed was its boiler.

There was a lot of activity close to the ship, and they hoped that meant it was preparing to leave soon.

It wasn't.

The captain, a portly middle-aged man who looked as if he survived on more than just the standard ship's rations, told them the ship needed a complete refit and he'd be lucky to leave in a month of Sundays.

'So why all the fuss and bother?' the Doctor asked, nodding at the activity round the ship.

'What, that? Because of the body.' Losing interest, the captain went back to his ship. Probably, Rose thought, to raid the fridge.

'Well, that just leaves the body,' the Doctor said

quietly. '*The body*,' he repeated in a doom-laden voice.

'"Leave well alone" wasn't a phrase they invented for you, was it?' Rose told him.

'Have psychic paper, will interfere. You have to do what you're good at.' He waved the wallet at her, and she guessed it would proclaim him as some high-ranking investigative official allowed access to anywhere in order to look at anything – whatever the people he showed it to thought was impressive.

It certainly worked. The various uniformed officials and paramedics moved aside to let them through to see the body.

'Why can't you use that to get good seats at a gig rather than to look at the gruesomes?' Rose muttered.

And it was gruesome. She looked away almost at once. But not quite quickly enough – not before she had seen the lacerated body, raked by sharp knives or claws. Not before she had seen the face frozen in terror. Not before she had seen that it was the old man, Rodd, who had spoken to them at the inn.

'Anything in the pockets?' the Doctor was asking, and Rose recalled how the man had reacted when he sorted through his money. 'A piece of paper perhaps? About so big, folded in half?'

'That's right, sir,' a voice said, surprised and impressed. 'I've got it right here. How did you know?'

'Lucky guess,' the Doctor said modestly. 'Show me.'

Rose turned to see. It had to be better than looking at the body. The Doctor was unfolding the piece of paper. Together they stared at the mark on it – a smudge of ink in the vague shape maybe of a figure.

'It's one of those tests, isn't it?' Rose suggested. 'See a butterfly and you're a nice person. See a bear and you've got problems.'

'What do you see?' the Doctor asked. His voice was grave.

'A black blob. Could be the shape of a man, I suppose.'

'I was afraid you'd say that.'

'Doesn't mean I'm a bad person. You seen this before?'

He shook his head. 'No. But I think it's what space sailors call the Black Shadow.'

'Sounds ominous.'

In the Doctor's palm, the paper was slowly yellowing, curling at the edges. As they watched it broke and crumbled and became dust. After a moment, even the dust was gone.

'It's a curse,' the Doctor said. 'You get given the Black Shadow and it means you're marked for death.'

'Oh, come on,' Rose blurted out. 'You can't be serious. No one believes that stuff these days.'

'No,' the Doctor said quietly, looking past Rose to where the body was being lifted on to a stretcher. 'Course they don't.'

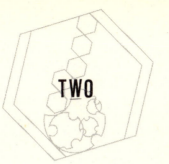

TWO

They watched as the body was loaded on to a small steam-driven cart. The official in charge – an officer of the Watch – was standing with them, obviously anxious to make a good impression. A dull grey man simpering in a dull grey uniform.

'Anything else I can do for you, sir?' he asked nervously as the cart puffed off along the quay.

'You do know the dead man was a friend of Drel McCavity?' the Doctor asked casually.

The officer went white. 'Er, no,' he admitted. 'A personal friend?'

'Well, acquaintance maybe. Someone ought to tell McCavity, don't you think?'

Rose hadn't thought the man could go any more pale, but somehow he managed it. 'Yes, sir,' he said hesitantly.

'Not some lackey, though. Not some junior officer sent along by a superior who's not got the stomach for it himself. Not having that.'

'Of course not, sir.' Even the man's voice had gone pale and faint now.

'Good man.' The Doctor clapped him on the shoulder. 'Knew you'd see it my way. Get me some transport, and I'll do it myself.'

The colour returned as quickly as it had gone. 'You, sir?' He made no effort at all to keep the relief out of his voice.

'Well, seems only fair.'

The officer nodded enthusiastic agreement and hurried off to organise transport.

'Is this a good idea?' Rose wondered aloud.

'Gets me in to see this McCavity bloke. Poor Rodd had been to see him, we know, so there's a reason to suppose McCavity will be interested. Plus he's rich and influential – might be able to get us on a ship. And they'll even deliver me to the door.'

'Hang on a minute – what do you mean "me"? What happened to "we"?'

'Oh, Rose, Rose, Rose,' he protested. 'How can you come when you'll be tracking down Rodd's other mates?'

'Edd and someone,' Rose remembered.

'Yeah. Edd and Bonny. There were four of them, and two are already dead.' He fluttered his fingers spookily and added in a deep voice, 'In mysterious circumstances.' Then he shrugged and stuffed his hands into his coat pocket. 'Someone needs to warn the other two, don't you think?'

'And how do I find them?'

'Well, if I knew that,' the Doctor told her in all apparent seriousness, 'if it was that easy, I'd do it myself.'

'Thanks a bunch.'

It was rather like a horse and cart, the Doctor decided. About as slow and as uncomfortable. The driver wore the same dull grey baggy uniform as the rest of the Watch. Like a London taxi driver, he seemed happy to talk about anything and everything rather than risk a single moment's peace and quiet. So the Doctor steered his monologue round to the subject of Drel McCavity.

'He keeps the place in order,' the driver said. 'We're well enough paid, as you know. Mind you, he can afford it, can't he? Now that Starfall is on the main mining routes and all. Not like the old days, when his dad bought this godforsaken lump of rock in the middle of nowhere. They said he was mad, but maybe he knew something no one else did. Maybe he could see what was coming. Or maybe it was just so cheap, what with the zeg and all.'

'Yes,' the Doctor said to prove he was still there and listening. 'The zeg.'

They were heading uphill now. The engine coughed and protested and struggled on the incline and the Doctor wondered if he ought to offer to get out and push. The metal-rimmed wheels clattered on the cobbled street. There were more people about now as the day got going. But the driver made no concessions, ignoring the dockers and children, who leaped out of the way of the vehicle.

The steam was blowing across the Doctor, bathing him in a warm, damp mist, and he pulled his coat closer about him.

'Not far now. But you know that, right. I mean, you must have met McCavity loads of times. What with you being the... a... whatever.'

'Must have,' the Doctor agreed.

The driver turned off the main street and on to a narrow roadway. The Doctor could see where they were heading now – an imposing stone-built house set away from the main community. It made him think of an old American plantation house. Imposing, prosperous, alone and aloof... Would its owner be the same?

'I've only been here the once before,' the driver was saying. 'Soon after I joined up. Sort of welcome-parade thing. Wasn't long after, you know... Might have been the first official function after that.'

'Really?' The Doctor wondered what he was talking about. It probably wouldn't take much to find out. 'So, how did it go?'

The driver grimaced. 'OK, I suppose. Till the end. Goofed then, didn't I? Got a right mashing from the captain afterwards. But how was I to know? I mean, no one warned me.'

'Well, quite. Not your fault. No one ever warns anyone about, you know, *that*. What happened?'

'He greeted us all by name. Impressive. The parade was on the lawn out the back of the house. And then we all trooped past, shaking his hand. And I just said it. Seemed like a good thing to say, and I meant it too.'

'I'm sure you did.'

'I said, "I'm so sorry about your wife." That was all. No more than that.' He sucked in a deep breath and shook his head. 'Bad move. I mean, yeah, she was his wife and, blimey, she was a beauty. But anyway…' The cart slowed to a steamy halt outside the impressive porch. 'They say he's just as touchy about it now as he ever was. And that was over ten years ago. Here you go, then, sir.'

The Doctor jumped down from the cart. 'Thanks for the ride.'

'Want me to wait?'

'That'd be kind.' The Doctor grinned at him in genuine gratitude. 'Yeah, thanks.'

Two large, uniformed guards with very obvious holsters were standing in the porch, watching the Doctor suspiciously. He smiled at them.

'The Doctor,' he announced to them. 'To see Mr McCavity. Official business,' he added, and flashed his psychic paper at them.

The two men blurred into action. One held the door open, while the other was already striding through the hallway in search of his master.

'In your own time,' the Doctor said happily.

Rose retraced her steps to the inn, but Silver Sally was gone. The young man who had taken her place behind the bar found time between pulling pints of grog to tell her that Sally worked nights. It was like being in a different place – so crowded and noisy now compared with the earlier quiet.

The girl serving at the tables was more helpful, and less bothered about keeping her customers waiting while she chatted to Rose. 'It's always like this when a shift changes,' she shouted above the noise. 'Oi – Telco, pipe down. Any trouble and I'll have the Watch on you, so help me.'

She knew Rodd and was saddened to hear of his 'accident', as Rose described it. She also knew Rodd's friends Edd and Bonny – all of them were regulars, it seemed – and she gave Rose directions to the warehouse she thought they currently worked in.

It didn't sound far. Rose thanked her, before shoving and pushing her way back out of the crowded bar. 'Good job it's not football night,' she muttered.

The guards had asked the Doctor to please wait in the hallway until Mr McCavity had time to see him. So it seemed only polite, the Doctor thought, to wait until they had gone before he wandered off to explore the house.

He wouldn't go far. Just a quick mooch round, get

his bearings, form an opinion of the owner from the property and furnishings… The first room he looked in was as grand and impressive as the hallway. Mid-colonial furnishings, pastel paint-job, nice carpet. And above the large stone fireplace was a portrait of a woman.

It was in a large, ornate, gold-leafed plaster frame, and had been painted by someone with more than a little talent. Even allowing for the fact that the artist might have been generous, the woman was a beauty. No denying it. She had a knowing half-smile on lips that were painted as blood-red as her velvet dress. Her dark hair was piled up on her head and her eyes were a startling green, staring out at the Doctor.

He gave the painted woman a little wave, checked no one was watching before blowing her a kiss, then went out again, pulling the door shut behind him.

The next room was smaller and more functional. It was dominated by a polished wooden desk. The top was clear apart from a small photo-frame, but this was evidently a study where someone worked. Pens and paper were arranged neatly on a side table, and there was a carafe of water next to them. Again there were pictures – dozens of them. Everywhere.

All of the same woman.

The framed photo on the desk was, not surprisingly, of the woman too. She was wearing the same blood-red dress as in the painting. Maybe it was a photo taken by the artist for reference.

Under the desk, almost out of sight, was a wooden chest. Bound with metal straps and held shut by a padlock it looked rather like an old sea chest, the Doctor thought. He tested the padlock, giving it a good tug, and felt the metal bracket give slightly. More for show than security, he decided – a good pull would wrench the thing open.

Across the other side of the hallway, the first door the Doctor tried led into a long gallery full of glass-fronted display cases. 'Whoa – now this is more like it,' he exclaimed, and peered into the first of the cabinets.

It contained a model of a spaceship. The sleek, matt-black hull and sophisticated laser-gun ports along the side seemed out of place in the wooden cabinet. A typewritten label described the ship as: '*Buccaneer* – the Feared Battle Cruiser of Notorious Space Pirate Hamlek Glint'. In smaller print it announced that the model had been built from the original blueprints and colour charts supplied by the Titan Spaceship Corporation. The final line on the card said: 'Present Whereabouts Unknown'.

The next case included bits of bent metal that were apparently from the cruise liner *Imperial*, which was destroyed in an attack by Glint after refusing to surrender. In pride of place were several charred pages from the ship's log, and a misshapen silicon chip that purported to be part of the main life-support system. It didn't look as if it would support an ant now.

There was something at the back of the case that the

Doctor could not quite make out. A picture, but faint like a watermark. Was it on the backcloth? A face? He looked closer, nose almost touching the glass. Funny – when he moved it seemed to disappear. And when he leaned away again it came back. Almost like a reflection.

'Ah,' he said in embarrassed realisation, and turned to smile apologetically at the man standing behind him. 'Drel McCavity, I presume.'

'You do presume. But yes, I'm McCavity. And you must be Doctor John Smith, Inspector of the Watch.'

'Yes, I must. Nice collection, by the way. Sorry to let myself in. Couldn't resist. Splendid stuff you've got here.'

'Thank you.' McCavity was a tall, thin man but with a deep bass voice. His hair was steel-grey although he looked to be in his early middle age – maybe in his mid-thirties. 'I thought I knew all the inspectors, but no matter. Let me show you round, Doctor.'

'Thanks, I'd like that. That's really kind.'

'While you tell me just why you're here. And why I've never heard of you.'

The third floor of the warehouse where Edd and Bonny were supposed to be working was dark and gloomy. Packing cases and wooden crates and pallets left little space for Rose to get through.

'Hello?' she shouted. Her voice echoed round, and got no reply.

She picked her way through the chaos, banging her ankle painfully on a crate and cursing under her breath.

'Anyone there?' she called again.

'Who wants to know?' a voice shouted back out of the gloom.

'I'm looking for Edd and Bonny.'

'Why?'

'Got a message for them.'

There was a pause. Rose was working her way slowly – and painfully as she caught her leg on another protruding edge – towards the voice.

'It's just a girl,' another voice said, quieter but just as gruff and abrupt.

'I'm not just a girl, I'm Rose. And I need to talk to you.'

A figure loomed up in front of her – dark and menacing. 'What about?'

Rose gulped. 'About Rodd. He's… There was an accident.'

'Accident, my elbow,' the other voice said from just behind her. 'He's dead, isn't he?'

'Yes,' she admitted. 'Sorry, but yes – yes, he is. You'd heard?'

The figure in front of Rose swore and sat down heavily on a crate. 'What happened?'

They all three sat down on crates, and as Rose's eyes adjusted to the dim light she could see that the dark figures were just ordinary men. Getting on in age, worn out by years of manual work, and frightened.

She told them all she knew.

'So the Doctor went to see this McCavity,' she finished. 'In case he's in danger too.'

'McCavity?' Edd said with a humourless laugh. 'Not likely. He can handle himself and no mistake.'

'He went intergalactic when he found out most of the stuff wasn't real,' Bonny agreed. 'Well, we knew it wasn't *really* Glint's. But it was the right period and all. Good stuff it was. No one would know. And we sold him some genuine stuff about ten years ago when we first came here. Really genuine, that was, so we thought he'd go for it.'

'Yeah, this stuff could easily have been Glint's,' Edd said. 'Can't tell, can you? I mean, no one's ever found his loot, so why not?'

'This stuff you sold McCavity,' Rose said, 'you were ripping him off.'

'No,' Edd protested. 'Well, not really. The medallion, all those years ago, that was real. He said to come back if we found anything else, though we never did. Been doing our stint on Maginot, haven't we? Till just recently. So this time we reckoned he'd be good for a few nice bits and pieces. Just a few trinkets. Some old coins, couple of jewels in a nice setting. Looked like pirate's treasure to us, and who's to say it wasn't?'

'Old Bobb, that's who,' Bonny replied. 'McCavity was happy enough to believe it was from Glint's haul till Bobb put him straight about it. He knew right away – knows his Glint, he does.'

'True,' Edd said. 'McCavity hadn't a clue. He kept on at us to say where we got it and if there was any more and what its provenance was. Couldn't very well tell him most of it came out of an old packing crate up here while we were clearing out, could we? Not and keep the customer happy. He wants cursed treasure, we'll do him cursed treasure.'

'Cursed, that's a laugh, isn't it?' Bonny said. 'Poor old Kaspar. And now Rodd as well. Reckon it's time to move on again. Someone don't like us.'

'McCavity?' Rose suggested.

Edd shrugged. 'Maybe. Got a temper on him, he has. But we gave him his money back.'

'Could be anyone,' Bonny said miserably. 'We've ripped off so many people in the past fifteen years, I forget.'

'Oh, charming,' Rose said to herself.

The sixth display case was empty. Or maybe it was the seventh. The Doctor stifled a yawn and pointed at the emptiness. 'Don't tell me, Hamlek Glint's invisibility cloak, right? Or is this reserved for the lost treasure?'

'Very amusing, Doctor,' McCavity said without the trace of a smile. 'By all accounts, the treasure wouldn't fit in there.'

'And the invisibility cloak?'

'Is hardly plausible.'

'Well, there's so much romance and fiction about it all, isn't there?'

'You mean the Resurrection Casket?'

The Doctor nodded, wondering what that might be. 'What else? Yes, that's exactly what I mean. Of course.'

'No, Doctor, this case contained some impressive artefacts which came into my possession recently. And which, even more recently, I discovered were not genuine relics from Glint's treasure at all. Despite the assurances I had been given.'

'Ah,' the Doctor realised. 'You mean by Rodd and his chums. Case of *caveat emptor*, was it? Let the buyer beware?'

'Indeed. Which brings us back to where we started, I think. I'm grateful for your concern about my well-being and safety, but I cannot believe that the poor man's death…'

'Poor men's deaths,' the Doctor corrected him coldly.

'I can't believe they have anything to do with the relationship I had with these blackguards.'

'Oh no?'

'No,' McCavity said emphatically. 'They sold me short. Possibly in good faith, though I doubt that. When confronted, they were happy to refund my money. Well…' A slight smile did now creep on to McCavity's face. 'Perhaps "happy" is not the right word.'

'But there were no hard feelings?'

'I didn't have them killed, if that's what you mean.'

Since that was exactly what the Doctor meant, he

smiled back. 'Nothing could have been further from my thoughts. Though someone had it in for that poor guy, didn't they?' He pointed to the next display case, only now having realised what was inside.

It was a screaming man. Or rather, it was a stylised metal sculpture of a man. He seemed to be covered in some viscous liquid that had poured over him and was now dripping and sliding down and off his body. The features were blurred and distorted, but the mouth was open and the eyes were wide in unmistakable terror.

'It's by Cathmann,' McCavity said, as if this explained everything. 'Depicting the death of Captain Lockhardt. His ship, the *Rising Moon*, held out against Glint for almost seventeen hours. That was his reward, according to the story. Covered in boiling lead as he tried to get to the escape pods.'

'Nasty,' the Doctor said quietly.

'You think so?' McCavity leaned forward, smiling. 'He thinks it's nasty, my love,' McCavity muttered to himself, so quietly that even the Doctor's keen hearing only just caught the sound. McCavity was still looking at the grotesque sculpture. 'I rather like it,' he said out loud.

'I meant it was nasty what happened to Lockhardt,' the Doctor told him. 'The sculpture is... extraordinary,' he agreed. 'Though I don't think *I* could ever say I liked it.'

'Well, that's a shame. But art all comes down to personal taste, doesn't it? Now, let me see you out.'

McCavity guided the Doctor towards the door.

The Doctor strained to look back over his shoulder, along the length of the gallery still unexplored. 'But there's so much more,' he protested, wondering what McCavity didn't want him to see.

'Another time, perhaps. I'm a busy man.'

They were out in the hall again. 'Will you wait here a moment?' McCavity asked.

'Why?'

McCavity frowned, just for a moment, then the smile was back. 'Let me give you my card. You can call me for a proper appointment and I can show you the rest of my collection.'

'Oh, I'm free most of the time,' the Doctor called after him, as McCavity headed for the door the Doctor knew led into the study.

'Call me,' he said again when he returned. He handed the Doctor a printed card – name and address, that was all.

'Thank you,' the Doctor said, stuffing the card into his trouser pocket. 'That's really very useful. Though I do know where you live.'

McCavity had his arm round the Doctor's shoulder, leading him to the door. 'He'll come back, darling,' McCavity muttered again, seeming not to notice that the Doctor had heard. 'Till next time, then, Doctor,' he added more loudly.

'As a hatter,' the Doctor said, nodding happily. 'Oh, one thing…'

'Yes?' The impatience was obvious in McCavity's tone.

'You didn't get angry with Rodd and the others, then?'

'Angry?'

'You know – miffed. Upset. Seething, furious, apoplectic. You didn't lose your temper with them?'

'I never lose my temper,' McCavity said levelly.

The door opened as they approached, one of the guards pushing it from the other side.

'Well, that's good,' the Doctor said. He smiled, and McCavity turned to go. He stopped, frozen, as the Doctor said, 'You know, I was *so* sorry about your wife.'

The hand of the guard closest to the Doctor moved towards his holster.

McCavity turned slowly back towards the Doctor. His face was white. He was shaking. His eyes burned with fury. When he spoke, his voice was also trembling as he struggled to keep it under control.

'She'll come back to me,' he said. He stepped forward, so his face was close to the Doctor's, their bodies almost touching. 'Be sure of that. She hasn't left me, not really. She'll be back. You'll see.'

'Oh, I do,' the Doctor replied quietly, sadly. 'Believe me, I do.'

'So, time to move on, then,' Edd was saying. He was just a dark shape against the pale orange from a grimy window on the far side of the warehouse floor.

Two dark figures, facing another two dark figures.

'The time has come,' Bonny agreed from beside Rose.

She frowned. Hang on – there were four of them now, how had that happened?

'The time has indeed come,' the figure beside Edd announced. The voice was deep and gruff and sounded slightly sad.

Edd gave a yelp of surprise and fear and leaped to his feet, Rose mirroring his movement. Bonny was standing up too – a knife glinting as he thrust it towards the newcomer.

The knife disappeared, swallowed by the enormous shaggy paw that grabbed it and wrenched it away. 'Well, can't sit here all day nattering,' the voice went on in a matter-of-fact tone, 'and, as you say, it's time. Sorry.'

Edd ran, with Rose close behind. She thought Bonny must be following too, but a choked-off cry of fright and pain burst that illusion. Rose skidded to a halt, wondering if she should go back and try to help.

And Edd's scream echoed in her ears from the other end of the warehouse.

Rose spun round. The huge, dark shape was lumbering towards her. Red eyes gleamed in the dim light. Something large and heavy flew past her and slumped across a nearby crate like a sack of potatoes. It was Edd.

'Don't let me keep you,' the monster said as it strolled past Rose. It gave her a cheery wave. 'Oh, and sorry about the mess.'

THREE

The driver was just as chatty on the way back from Drel McCavity's. 'He still talking to himself as much?'

'Oh yes,' the Doctor assured the man.

'Muttering and murmuring to his long-lost love. I heard of one officer who thought McCavity was talking to him and answered a question he wasn't meant to have heard.'

'Embarrassing,' the Doctor sympathised.

'Painfully so,' the driver agreed quietly, and uncharacteristically he offered no further details. 'So, how d'you get on with McCavity, then?' he asked when he eventually seemed in danger of grinding to a conversational halt.

'Brilliant,' the Doctor replied. 'Marvellous. Really hit it off. Couldn't have gone better. Good one.'

The Doctor had asked the driver if he knew where Bobb lived. Not surprisingly, he did. It was at the end of a narrow cobbled street the other side of the docks, in the shadow of an enormous crane. The Doctor watched clouds of steam puffing out from the side of the crane as it swung and lifted and lowered.

'Want me to wait?' the driver asked as the Doctor thanked him and climbed down.

'No, I'll take it from here, thanks all the same.'

'You need me, just ask for Big Jessie.'

The Doctor looked up at him. 'Big Jessie,' he repeated in a level tone.

'You got it.'

The Doctor grinned. 'I'll do that, thanks.' He waved the driver goodbye. 'Big Jessie,' the Doctor repeated under his breath as the cart steamed off along the street. Then he turned and pulled the bell cord hanging by the door.

'Doctor.' Bobb seemed surprised to see him so soon, but the Doctor smiled winningly and invited himself inside.

'I've just been chatting to a friend of yours.'

'Oh?' Bobb seemed bemused.

'Drel McCavity.'

'Oh. Hardly a friend. We share an interest.'

'Yes. I gather you pointed out to him recently that he'd made a less than inspired purchasing decision.'

'You what?' Bobb led the way through to the small living room.

The Doctor was looking round with interest. The house was not big, but it was full of Glint artefacts. Not like McCavity's, where they were in a separate gallery, but everywhere – antiques that the Doctor assumed were connected with Glint stood on every surface. There were paintings and pictures of Glint's ship and her crew hanging on every wall. He paused to inspect what looked almost like a class photo – only with a difference.

'He bought some fake Glint artefacts,' the Doctor said.

'Oh, that. Yeah – he should have spotted them a mile off. Wasn't too happy when I told him.' Bobb seemed amused at the memory.

'Lucky he never loses his temper, then,' the Doctor said quietly. He tapped the glass over the picture. 'You know, I didn't realise about Glint's crew. Were they all robots?'

They stood together looking at the picture. It showed a group of figures standing outside the main hatch of Glint's ship. The figure in the middle was evidently Glint himself – a tall, broad-shouldered man with black hair and an enormous beard. His eyes gleamed greedily even through the sepia tint of the picture.

Kneeling at Glint's feet was a boy of about fifteen. But none of the other figures were human. The Doctor counted. Seven robots – gleaming, metallic, angular and brutal-looking. They were all of different design, but all were obviously built for combat. The one on Glint's left was shorter than its captain by a head, but almost as broad. Its left arm ended in a vicious-looking blade. The face was a blank mask of metal with gaping dark eyes and mouth, like a skull…

'That's Robbie, the cabin boy.' A small finger reached out and pointed at the kneeling figure. The finger belonged to Jimm. He had managed to push between the Doctor and Bobb without being noticed.

'Do you know the names of the robots too?' the Doctor asked.

'Oh yes. I know them all.' He pointed to the squat shape beside Glint. 'That's Salvo 7-50. The tall mark-three battle robot behind is Cannon-K. I've got an old action figure of him. Uncle Bobb doesn't like me playing with it because it's quite rare. You're supposed to keep it in the box and not use it, then it's more valuable. But I think it should be played with. I've got them all, but Cannon-K's the only one from the original set, when they first came out.'

The Doctor leaned slightly closer. 'You carry on playing with it,' he whispered. 'Because, know what? You're right, that's what toys are for.'

'Have to get Bobb to mend it again first, though,' Jimm said sadly. 'The head keeps coming off. We glue it back on, but the neck's really thin. I think it's a design flaw, but Bobb says the figure's really accurate. Not like the junk you get free these days with kronkburgers on Salarius. Or so Bobb says.'

The Doctor smiled at Bobb over Jimm's head. Bobb was watching Jimm, the affection he felt for his nephew apparent as he ruffled the boy's hair. 'You got a toy of this one too, then?' the Doctor asked, pointing to another of the robots.

Jimm nodded. 'That's Elvis,' he said. The robot the Doctor was pointing to seemed to have flared metal legs and painted eyebrows. 'No one knows why he was called that.'

'And this one?' The Doctor pointed to what looked like an oil drum with stubby legs and machete-tipped arms.

'Got him too. That's Dusty. And that one is Stubbs.' Jimm was tapping his finger on a bulky robot that had caterpillar tracks instead of feet and very short arms. Its electronic camera-eyes stared out from the middle of its chest. 'Next to him is Octo 1-9, that one with all the segmented arms with different attachments. You get some of the different attachments with the action figure, though they're really small and I've lost most of them. And last of all is Smithers.' The final robot seemed to be leaking dark fluid all down its front. Apart from that it looked like a fairly respectable metal and plastic representation of a man.

'Last and least,' Bobb said. 'He was the engineer. Worked below decks most of the time.'

'Last?' the Doctor said. 'Then who's that?' He pointed to the final figure – a large, dark silhouette, the detail lost in the shadows at the edge of the picture.

'It's no one,' Bobb said. 'Just a shadow. The way the light falls.'

The Doctor peered at the picture. 'Are you sure? Looks like a person. Someone big and scary.' He puffed out his chest and swung his arms by way of demonstration. 'Another pirate maybe,' he said in an artificially deep voice.

'No,' Jimm assured him. 'It's no one. That was Glint's crew. Robbie and seven robots. Till he betrayed them.'

'Oh, great – there's a story. What happened?'

'No one knows what happened to Robbie,' Bobb told him. 'Probably got dumped out of an airlock, poor kid. Glint sold the robots to a droid dealer on Metallurgis Five. For scrap.'

'They were melted down the same day,' Jimm said. 'That's the story. And Glint sailed off towards Starfall and was never seen again.'

On the other side of the room was a framed star map. Bobb walked briskly over to it and pointed to Starfall, at the bottom right edge of the map. 'Glint could never have got here.' He indicated a shaded area that covered the whole left side of the map. 'That's the zeg. His ship would have packed up as soon as he got to the Outreaches. He probably headed off in a completely different direction, truth be known. But it makes a good story. Lost treasure. Need something to keep people coming here.'

'A good story,' the Doctor mused. 'Is that why you're so fascinated with it?'

'As good a reason as any,' Bobb said.

The doorbell rang before the Doctor could reply, and Jimm ran to see who it was. The Doctor took the opportunity to ask Bobb, 'If you're so mad keen on

Glint and the romance and the swashbuckling and the lure of the spaceways…'

'Why am I so down on Jimm when he wants to find out more? Why don't I encourage his boyish enthusiasm?'

The Doctor nodded and stabbed the air with his index finger. 'Exactly.'

'I'm not a romantic, Doctor. Not like Drel McCavity. He's really drawn by the stories of the lost treasure and the casket and everything. My interest is more academic, I suppose. I'm a historian. And I have a regard for the truth behind the legend. I know it wasn't all excitement and heroism and derring-do.'

'No,' the Doctor agreed quietly, 'it wasn't.'

'People died,' Bobb said, and the Doctor was surprised to see there was real sadness in his eyes. 'For all the adventure and the adrenaline, Glint was a murderer. Oh, he didn't set out to kill people just for the hell of it – though I think Salvo and some of the other droids probably did. But if they got in the way of the wealth, if it cost a few people's lives to get a little bit richer…' He shrugged. 'Never mind the piracy and the theft and the looting. Hamlek Glint didn't value *life*. That was his real crime. And I don't want Jimm growing up with that attitude. For every blaster and laser-sabre and depleted trisilicate cannon shell I have in my collection, I remember the people it killed.'

'That won't bring them back,' the Doctor said gently.

'But it might keep others alive.'

The Doctor nodded. He was beginning to understand. And Bobb looked as if he wanted to talk. There were tears welling up in his eyes. The Doctor smiled sadly. 'Who did *you* lose?' he asked quietly.

But before Bobb could reply, the door opened and Jimm was back, with Silver Sally.

'Look who's come to visit us,' the boy said excitedly.

And the moment was lost.

It didn't surprise Rose that there was no Doctor and no message for her at the inn. But the same girl who had given her directions to the warehouse told her the way to Bobb's house. If she thought Rose seemed flustered and pale and nervous, she didn't mention it.

The atmosphere at Bobb's, when Rose got there, could hardly be said to match her mood. There were two people lying dead in a warehouse and not only had she done nothing to prevent their deaths, she hadn't even told anyone. But she was only too aware that Edd and Bonny were beyond her help and if she tried to tell the officers of the Watch what had happened she might well end up taking the rap herself. So it was both calming and frustrating to find the Doctor sitting with Bobb, Jimm and Silver Sally, drinking what seemed uncannily like tea, eating what seemed suspiciously like fruit cake and telling stories of courage on the final frontier that sounded implausibly improbable even to Rose. The Doctor was talking in his 'almost laughing' tone of voice – as if he was on the edge of finishing an outrageously funny joke and struggling not to break into hysterics.

'There's this apologetic monster,' she blurted at the first pause in the Doctor's monologue, 'ripping people apart and saying how sorry he is about it.'

The Doctor looked at her. 'Blimey,' he said. 'Well, that's a new one. Have a cuppa and tell us all about it in a minute when I've finished explaining about Ferdy the Fanatic.'

'There's people dead, Doctor,' she protested loudly.

'Yes, and that's the point.' He wasn't even looking at her, he was talking to Jimm, and the laughter had faded from his voice. 'For all the excitement and adventure and really wild things going on, the danger was always very real. Ferdy was real. He *really* died. There's a cost, when you wish for things there's always a cost. You have to make sure it's a price you're willing to pay. And life is the highest price of all. Isn't that right, Rose?' he added quietly.

Rose nodded, unable for a moment to speak as she realised he wasn't just telling stories.

Old Bobb seemed to have realised that too, because he reached across the table and clasped the Doctor's hand in his own for a moment. 'Thanks,' he said, nodding solemnly.

'Now then, monsters!' The Doctor was on his feet, walking round the table so they all had to turn – and continue turning back and forth to keep him in sight as he paced up and down and paused to bounce enthusiastically on the balls of his feet. 'This creature will have gone by now, and we can't do anything for his victims apart from get blamed for their deaths, which won't help anybody.' He tapped his knuckles against his teeth. 'Have my fingers always been this long?' he wondered aloud. 'Never mind.' His long index finger was pointing at Rose now. 'Dead people – friends of previous victims?'

'Yeah. So there's a connection, right?'

'Right. Has to be. So what do the victims have in common apart from knowing each other? Starter for ten, anyone?'

Jimm was listening, wide-eyed.

Silver Sally's shoulder joint hissed and steamed as she leaned across the table towards Rose. 'Edd and Bonny?'

Rose nodded.

'Some scam, then,' Sally said. She shrugged, as if dismissing them. 'They probably asked for it.'

Bobb sighed. 'I'm afraid I'd have to agree. Not *really* bad guys, but always on the take. Always ripping people off. Taking and selling what wasn't theirs.'

'Like fake Glint artefacts?' the Doctor asked. 'To Drel McCavity?'

'Ah,' said Bobb. 'Yes, you know about that, don't you?'

The Doctor nodded. 'Hey, tell me, what did happen to McCavity's wife? It obviously left a deep impression on him.'

'Hey, tell me,' Rose echoed, mimicking, 'when did this conversation go completely whoosh.' She waved her hand over her head. 'I mean like, what are you talking about?'

They started from basics, with Bobb and Jimm giving Rose, the Doctor and Sally a tour of Bobb's collection. Rose had expected a few odds and ends in a shoebox, so a 'tour' was rather more than she had bargained for.

'Who was this Glint bloke, then?' she asked as Bobb led them through to a long, narrow gallery.

The gallery was lined with display cases and pictures. The display cases held guns and instruments and bits of metal the purpose of which Rose couldn't even begin to guess at. All were old and tarnished, and many were twisted and broken. The pictures were of spaceships – some new and pristine, some old wrecks ripped apart by cannon fire. There were ships' manifests listing cargo and passengers, framed newsprint reports of attacks and destruction. Several tailors' dummies stood round wearing old clothes – overalls smeared with oil, a futuristic ship's captain's tunic with lots of gold braid, a ball gown with a hole burned through it…

'Hamlek Glint,' Bobb was saying. 'The Scourge of the Spaceways. He was a pirate, a privateer, an adventurer, a bandit… He stole a fortune in jewels, precious metals and rare artefacts in a career that lasted over fifty years.'

'And what happened to him in the end?' Rose asked. 'Was he caught?'

'Never,' Sally said. 'He was too clever for the Space Revenue Directorate. Him and his crew. SRD never got close.'

'And his crew were robots, right?' the Doctor said.

Bobb nodded. 'All except the cabin boy and…' His voice tailed off as he paused to wipe a speck of dust from the captain's tunic.

'And?' Rose prompted.

'And that was probably why he was so successful. They were a cut-throat bunch, all with faulty personality circuits that should have been recalled and impounded for violating the First Law. But they worked as a team, and they respected Glint absolutely, trusted him completely.'

'Ironic, really,' Sally said.

'Oh – why?' Rose asked.

'Because he sold them for scrap,' Jimm said. 'That's the story. You wanted to know what happened to Glint. He was never caught, he vanished. Sold his crew to a tech yard on Metallurgis Five, sailed off into the spiral and was never seen again.'

'But why?'

'P'raps he got a good retirement package,' the Doctor said. 'No pension plan problems I'm guessing – right?'

'Right. He had a fortune amassed by then and no mistake,' Bobb said.

'Come and see it,' Jimm said excitedly. 'The Lost Treasure. We've got it through here.' He was skipping on ahead, beckoning to them to follow. His enthusiasm was infectious and the others all hurried to catch up.

'You've got Glint's fortune?' Sally was saying.

'Not really,' Bobb said, smiling. 'Just a mock-up of what it might have looked like, stacked in his hold. Call it sculpture, if you prefer. Had a chap come in and put it together from old tin cans and metal foil and stuff years ago, using photos and lists of what Glint stole for reference. It's not terribly convincing, to be honest. But Jimm likes it.'

To Rose, it looked exactly as she imagined a pile of treasure looted from rich cargo ships and passenger space liners of the future would look. She joined the others to peer through a glass screen into a small room that seemed to be piled high with ingots and jewels, gold and silver, coins and antiques.

'Mmm, I see what you mean,' the Doctor said, evidently less impressed. 'Is that an old raffle ticket I can see down there?'

'It looks very good to me,' Sally said.

'It's great,' Jimm assured her.

Bobb smiled indulgently. 'Not so convincing up close, I'm afraid. I have to keep the environment sealed and airtight or some of the materials the chap used will decay and tarnish.'

'Might spoil the effect,' the Doctor agreed. 'I'm

getting to be quite an expert on Glint exhibitions, you know. This is my second today.'

They turned to move on. All but Jimm. 'There's some Five Alzarian Sestertii coins missing,' he said. 'Look, Uncle Bobb – on that low shelf at the back. There was a whole pile of them, a dozen at least. Now there's only a few.'

Bobb turned back to look, frowning. 'I don't think so, lad,' he said, ruffling the boy's hair with his hand. 'Your eyes are bigger than the treasure.'

'No,' Jimm insisted. 'There's some missing.'

'Slipped down maybe,' the Doctor offered. 'Fallen off the shelf perhaps. Had any earthquakes recently? Troupe of Morris dancers strutting their stuff upstairs perchance?'

The next room was taken up with blackened, broken pieces of spaceship. Fuselage housings, hull plates and engine components from the exterior; furnishings, lamps and fixtures from the interior.

'All that is left of the *Nova Princess*,' Bobb said.

Rose was standing beside the Doctor. 'Y'know, this house seems bigger inside than out,' she said.

'If it really was,' the Doctor replied, 'that'd give us something to worry about. What's special about the *Nova Princess*?' he asked loudly. 'Apart from the fact people died?'

'Last of Glint's conquests,' Jimm told them. 'Last liner he hit before he sold his crew and vanished into space.'

'And remind me, why do people think he came to Starfall?'

'They don't,' Sally said. 'He was just heading this way.'

'It's only a story,' Bobb agreed. 'Maybe he *was* heading this way. Maybe he really had got to the point where he'd had enough of it all and just wanted to retire and put his feet up. Maybe he was sick of the death and the killing and the constant running and hiding. I don't expect we'll ever know. As I told the Doctor before, he didn't have a steamship, so he couldn't have come here.'

'And what sort of ship *did* he have?' Rose asked.

'The *Buccaneer* was a battle cruiser, wasn't it?' the Doctor said. 'Astra class, from the design of the exhaust intakes.'

Bobb nodded.

'How d'you know that, then?' Rose asked.

'Drel McCavity had a model of it. Which reminds me,' he said to Bobb, 'you were going to tell me what happened to McCavity's wife.'

'She vanished too,' Sally said. 'Not much mystery there, though. Ran off with the Captain of the Watch.'

'Happens,' the Doctor said.

'Everyone knew they were seeing each other,' Bobb agreed. 'Everyone except Drel. I don't think he had an inkling until they'd gone. He took it very badly.'

'He's still taking it very badly from what I saw. What I heard. Wonder if it's the fact she left him or the fact everyone else knew and he didn't that rankles the most.'

Bobb led them out of the room and back to the living room. 'Probably the latter,' he said. 'He's an obsessive sort of chap. After Larissa left him, he became obsessed with the Glint legends. That's when he started collecting, though I think a lot of it is for the publicity.'

'You what?' Rose said.

'A lot of people come through Starfall, go on to the belt and the mines because of the Glint legends,' Sally told them. 'If you've got the choice of mining in Scotia, which is pretty grim but they aren't in the zeg, or round here, where there's no power or chip technology, then most people would go for Scotia. But if you think there's a chance to find a massive haul of hidden treasure, that could sway your choice.'

'And McCavity gets a percentage of everything that goes through here, right?' Rose remembered.

'Right,' the Doctor said. 'So he's promoting industry and tourism. Well, industry anyway. And because he's less of an expert and more of an obsessive he's easy prey to anyone who has an old bit of junk they claim is something to do with Glint.'

'Like the dead blokes,' Rose realised.

'Like, as you say, the dead blokes.'

'Well,' Bobb said slowly, 'he's not daft. He's not someone you want to upset. And he knows what he doesn't know, so he usually asks my professional opinion. If nothing else it makes me a few shillings here and there. Only this time he'd already bought the stuff before I could look at it for him.'

'That's right,' Jimm chipped in. 'You couldn't just take him an old wooden box and claim it's the Resurrection Casket.'

'Another myth?' the Doctor prompted.

Bobb nodded. 'It was what made Glint so fearsome to his enemies. No one knows how the stories started, or even if they had any truth in them. But the Resurrection Casket was said to be his greatest find.'

'"Find" as in "finders, keepers", meaning he stole it?' Rose checked.

'From a Cryonoflast clone ship, so the story goes.'

'And this Resurrection Casket thing is what exactly? Dead bodies in a coffin or something?' Rose asked.

'It is said that the casket could contain the soul after death.'

'And when you open the casket,' Jimm said excitedly, 'the person is brought back to life again. So if Glint was wounded or dying, or killed even, then they could just stick him in the Resurrection Casket and he'd come back to life.'

'A foe who can't be killed,' the Doctor mused. 'Yeah, that'd put the fear of Skaro into you, wouldn't it?'

'If the Resurrection Casket ever really existed,' Bobb said quietly. 'And if it really did what people think.'

Sally had left and Jimm was helping Bobb clear away

the tea things. 'This isn't helping us get the TARDIS working again,' Rose told the Doctor when she managed to draw him to one side and speak to him in private.

'Fun, though,' the Doctor countered. 'Hey, there's something I want you to see. Come on.'

'Where?' she asked anxiously.

'Just over here.' He led her to the door and showed her a picture hanging on the wall. 'That's the notorious Glint, together with his crew.' He pointed out Robbie the cabin boy and then each of the robots in turn, finishing with 'Salvo 7-50 – the fiercest and most vicious pirate of the lot. Ha-ha!' he added for good measure, in what might have been a deep Cornish accent.

'Yeah, I've been thinking about that, and about this casket thing.'

'Oh?'

'And if Glint lives for ever, right…'

'That isn't quite what the story says,' the Doctor pointed out.

'No, OK, but he vanished, yeah? And he might have come here. And Bobb knows a hell of a lot about it all.' She leaned closer, examining the man in the picture, her voice almost a whisper. 'You can't really tell, what with the beard and everything, but suppose, just suppose…'

'That Bobb is really Hamlek Glint?' the Doctor whispered back, wide-eyed.

'Yeah. Well, why not?'

The Doctor was grinning, and that didn't fill Rose with confidence in her theory. 'Because,' he said, 'Bobb must be what – about sixty? Just because he's collecting all this Glint stuff doesn't mean anything.'

'Yeah, but Glint looks about, what, mid-forties in the picture. And maybe that was taken soon before he vanished.'

'Maybe it was. But even so, Rose – Glint vanished nearly fifty years ago.'

'Oh.'

'And he was human, no one seems to doubt that. So if he is still around, then the only thing he's collecting is his pension, and he's probably having to be wheeled in to get that.'

'Oh,' Rose said again. 'So what are we looking at?'

The Doctor pointed to the edge of the picture. 'This. See it? That dark patch.'

'Shadows?' She peered closely at it. 'Or maybe a figure. Difficult to tell.'

'Remind you of anything?'

He had an eyebrow raised in that meaningful way that told her she was missing something. So she looked again. And now she did see it. 'It looks like…'

'Yes?'

'A dark, shaggy figure. Like the monster that attacked Edd and Bonny.'

'Yeah, I was afraid you'd say that,' the Doctor said sadly.

'I think it's the Black Shadow,' a voice said from somewhere below the picture.

Rose and the Doctor both looked down in surprise, and found that Jimm was standing there.

'You been there long?' the Doctor demanded.

He didn't answer. He was pointing at the dark patch in the picture. 'Don't you think it looks like the Black Shadow? You know the old sailors' curse. Get the Black Shadow put on you and you're marked for death.'

Rose was staring wide-eyed at the Doctor. 'Like the paper that man had!'

'What man?' Jimm asked. But at that moment the doorbell went. 'I'll get it,' he called, and raced off.

'He's all excitement and enthusiasm, that kid,' the Doctor said. He shook his head in admiration. 'Imagine what it is to be young, eh.' Then he caught Rose's expression and his smile faded. 'Sorry. Younger. I mean, well, you're young, of course, and you have imagination, no denying that, but… Yeah, the Black Shadow.' He cleared his throat. 'I suppose it looks a bit like it. From memory, the Black Shadow looks like this.' He stuffed his hands into his coat pockets. 'Right, paper, must have some paper somewhere. Drel McCavity's business card, and… What's this?'

Along with the card he had pulled a folded slip of paper from his pocket.

Rose barely heard the sound of the front door opening from out in the hallway.

She was watching the Doctor unfold the paper.

Then she heard Jimm's scream.

She saw the dark shape that had already been drawn on the paper the Doctor was holding and was staring at. 'Ye-ah,' he was saying slowly. 'The Black Shadow looks *exactly* like that.' He gave a low whistle. 'That's clever, that is.'

And an enormous shaggy figure, black as a moonless night, filled the doorway beside them.

'Not you again!' a gruff voice said to Rose. 'This is becoming a habit. Look, I'm really sorry about this.'

The Doctor was holding up the paper, as if to compare the shape on it with the shape in the doorway. As a huge paw tipped with long, sharp claws slashed down towards him.

FOUR

At the last possible moment, the Doctor stepped aside, and the massive paw slashed down on empty space.

'Now we're really getting somewhere,' he told Rose in breathless excitement. Then he ran.

'Yeah, like the morgue,' she said under her breath. 'Oh, sorry,' she added, out of habit, as the monster gently eased her aside so it could get through the door and chase after the Doctor. It was at least eight feet tall, and Rose caught the musty animal smell of it as she moved.

'Excuse me,' it said. 'Ta. See you next time maybe,' it added as it crossed the room in long, lumbering strides.

The Doctor had disappeared through the door that led into Bobb's exhibition area, while the creature paused by a mirror. It inspected its reflection briefly, before breathing heavily on its claws and polishing them on its fur.

'You'd better not have hurt that boy,' Rose shouted after it.

The expression the creature gave her as it paused to look back was pained. 'Please, what do you take me for?' It shook its head, tutted, clicked its tongue, and was gone.

'And you'd better not hurt the Doctor, neither,' Rose shouted, unsure whether to follow the monster or check that Jimm really was OK. 'Oh, the Doctor can look after himself,' she decided. 'I expect.' And ran to find Jimm.

It was not in the Doctor's nature to run away. What he really wanted was a way of negotiating from a position of strength. A sophisticated and terrible weapon of some sort to defend himself with. A long pointed stick would be a start. He didn't want to hurt the creature, but there were some questions he'd like answered. And it would be nice too, he was thinking, if he could avoid getting killed.

Through the room full of surviving artefacts from the *Nova Princess* and out past the treasure room. There was a dark, narrow passage down the side of the large glass panel protecting the treasure. The Doctor dived into it, hoping the creature close behind him was too large to follow.

He moved slowly, cautiously, quietly along the passage, and found it ended in a blank wall, with a door leading off to the side. Probably locked, but he tried the handle anyway and, to his surprise, the door opened.

Glancing back along the passage, the Doctor could see the monster's shaggy form silhouetted in the viewing area beyond. It didn't seem to have realised where the Doctor had gone. So long as he did nothing silly, he should be able to slip away. He backed slowly and quietly into the dimly lit room beyond the door.

Straight into the pile of 'treasure'. A stack of silver goblets, balanced against large gold plates, toppled over and crashed noisily down, dragging other artefacts and jewels and coins and relics in an avalanche to the floor.

'Cripes,' the Doctor said out loud, watching the cascade. 'Air-tight seal, my elbow.' Then he frowned. 'That's interesting.' His eyes followed the path of a brooch apparently inlaid with rubies and seemingly studded with diamonds as it skittered to a halt. Someone else was watching too, he realised. Through the glass panel. The monster was standing with its paws on its hips and its head tilted to one side, staring right back at him.

'How not to attract attention, lesson one,' the Doctor muttered. He waved.

The monster waved back. Then it leaped at the glass and crashed on through, coming straight at the Doctor.

But the Doctor wasn't there. He was running back down the passage and out past the smashed window into the long gallery of display cases. There on the gallery wall, just as he remembered, was a laser blaster.

It was old and corroded and he had the devil's own job yanking it from the bracket that held it in place. But as the monster arrived at the end of the gallery, the Doctor was ready. He held the gun steady, aiming from the hip.

The monster paused, perhaps unsure, looking down the barrel.

'No closer, or I fire,' the Doctor said, his voice stern and menacing.

The monster laughed. 'Oh, do me a favour.'

'This blaster might look old and rusty and naff, but I can assure you it's in perfect working order.'

'Probably is,' the monster agreed, starting slowly down the gallery towards him. 'Go on, then – have a go.'

The Doctor aimed high and to the left, so the first laser bolt would go over the monster's shoulder. A warning shot. He squeezed the trigger. Nothing happened. Nothing except the slow, sickly, sinking feeling in the pit of his stomach.

'Oh, zeg! Zegging hell!' The Doctor threw the useless blaster down on the floor.

'I hope you haven't broken that,' the monster told him seriously. 'That's Bobb's. He's very proud of that.'

'Is he really?' The Doctor stood his ground. 'And what do you care? You're going to rip this place apart to get at me anyway.'

'Oh, come on, that's not fair,' the monster protested. It was standing right in front of the Doctor now, towering above him. 'Rip *you* apart, yeah – I mean, that's what I have to do. But I can't be doing with mess and damage and needless vandalism. No, really. I mean, given the choice I wouldn't rip anything up at all.' It seemed to shrug, massive shoulders moving sympathetically. 'Job's a job, though. Sorry about that.' It reached down and clamped a paw on each of the Doctor's shoulders, squeezing hard.

'Hang on, hang on,' the Doctor said quickly, wincing. 'Are you saying that you would rather not kill me?'

'Well, on balance. I suppose…'

'But that you have to.'

'Black Shadow. It's like a contract. Don't have a choice really. Either I do the business or I get the treatment in return. Whack! Off back to where I came from, for an eternity of pain and suffering.'

'And where's that? Where you come from, I mean?'

'The Black Shadow Dimension.'

The Doctor gave as close an approximation to a nod as he could under the circumstances. 'Of course. That figures.'

'So, sorry. Ready for this?'

'Oh, I've been ready for about a hundred and fifty…' The Doctor's voice faded as a thought struck him. 'Wait a sec.'

The monster sighed. 'What is it now?'

'How do you know it's me you want?'

'I got a name, a description, and an uncanny ability to detect the Black Shadow parchment from the way it resonates between the dimensions due to the precise polygonal structure of the shape and the molecular composition of the ink. Never made a mistake yet.' It thought about this, then added, 'Not that I know of anyway.'

'But you don't enjoy this?'

'What, ripping people's heads off and all that?'

'Yeah. And all that. You're not really that keen, are you? I can tell.'

'No choice, though,' the monster said sadly. 'So, if you'll just hold still.' It tightened its grip and there was an ominous creaking and cracking sound.

'No, no, no!' The Doctor's teeth clenched. 'You've got the wrong person.'

The grip relaxed a little. 'Really? No, I suppose,' it went on, considering, 'given the choice I'd rather take some time out, relax a bit, catch up on the vids I've missed. And I've got a stack of books as high as your head that I haven't got round to reading. High as your head at the moment anyway. Could even maybe do another degree.'

The Doctor was struggling to pull free. 'What?' he asked in amazement.

'I know, I know,' the monster admitted. 'I mean, what would I do with it? I've got three already. And an honorary doctorate.'

'Really?' This was a ray of hope. 'Me too. Well, sort of. What a small universe. You know, you and me have so much in common.'

'Neither of us with a future in this dimension, you mean?'

'That's right. Er, no,' the Doctor corrected himself. 'No, that's not what I meant. You've got the wrong person – trust me!'

'Why?'

'Because you don't really want to kill me.' The Doctor's feet had left the ground and he was wondering if he'd ever feel them touch it again.

'True. But, like I said, no choice. Sorry.'

'And I can prove it.'

The monster slowly lowered the Doctor back down. 'Oh?'

'Whoever put the Black Shadow on me – you know, old, er, what's his name…'

The monster laughed again. 'Nah, you won't get me like that. Not able to divulge my master's name. Or is she maybe a mistress? Sorry. Do that, and you could maybe slip the Black Shadow back to them and reverse the curse so I have to kill them. Which, let's face it, would let you off the hook but I'm strictly forbidden from helping. You know? Sorry.' The paws were digging into the Doctor's shoulder again. 'Nice coat, by the way. I'll try not to spoil it.'

'Oh, thanks. But, wait, you said you had my name.'

'So?'

'What is it?'

'You don't know your own name? What are you on about – is this some "don't let me die in ignorance" ploy? If so, you should know I've heard them all in my time. There was this one guy, you know – and you'll never credit it – but he actually –'

'No,' the Doctor protested. 'No, that's not it. If they gave you my name, then you've got the wrong person.' Pain was shooting through his shoulders and down his arms and the world had tilted to an alarming angle as the monster raised him above its head. He scrabbled and tore at the monster's fur, but to little effect. 'I don't have a name!' the Doctor shouted. 'That's me – the Doctor with no name. Ask anyone.'

In the distance, the Doctor could hear Rose shouting for him: 'Doctor!'

'You see,' he told the patch of fur closest to him.

The world paused in mid-spin for a moment. 'No name?'

'That's right. Just "The Doctor". That's not a name, is it?'

'No kidding.'

The world tilted again and the Doctor assumed the monster was being sarcastic. He assumed the last thing he would ever be aware of was the pungent smell of its shaggy body. That, somehow, didn't seem very fair.

But then he was back on his feet, large hairy paws dusting down his lapels for him, then slapping him on the bruised shoulder. 'No name,' the monster said again, shaking its head. 'Well, there's a thing. Bit of a sad thing actually, when you think about it. Well, obviously there's been a mix-up somewhere. I'm really sorry about that. Misunderstanding. Hope you don't bear a grudge.'

'Not at all,' the Doctor managed to gasp. 'I hope I haven't put you out, er…'

'Kevin,' the monster said. 'Nice to meet you, Doctor.' It let out a guffaw of laughter. 'Doctor No Name.'

'It's not that funny,' the Doctor said. 'Kevin.'

The monster was wandering back down the gallery, fading slowly from existence – back to the Black Shadow Dimension presumably. It waved cheerily as it went. 'Remember me to your blonde friend.' Then it was gone, the Doctor staring at the space where it wasn't, and shaking his head in a mixture of relief, disbelief, pain and amusement.

Which was how Rose found him when she skidded into the room moments later. Staring into space and rubbing his shoulders like he was hugging himself.

'Where's your apologetic friend?' she asked.

'What?' He turned towards her, looking thoughtful. 'Oh, you mean Kevin.'

She just stared back at him. 'Kevin?'

'Yeah. Nice enough chap. Had some reading to catch up on. Or something.'

'You're kidding, right?'

'Not at all. He said to remember him to you.'

'Thanks.'

The Doctor grinned, and suddenly Rose knew he was all right.

'I think Kevin fancies you actually,' the Doctor said.

'It all connects back to Hamlek Glint,' the Doctor announced a few minutes later.

'What does?' Bobb asked.

The four of them were gathered in the living room of Bobb's house. Three of them – Rose, Jimm and Bobb himself – were sitting down. The Doctor was wired, pacing round the room, pausing to examine pictures and maps and a milk jug left from tea.

'Everything.' He put the milk jug down on the table. 'The artefacts McCavity bought.'

'Fake,' Rose pointed out.

'Fake Glints,' the Doctor countered. 'Then there's the Black Shadow.' He whirled round and pointed at Jimm. 'Tell me, did Glint ever put the Black Shadow on his enemies?'

'All the time,' Jimm said. 'Famous for it. Anyone who betrayed him, they got the Black Shadow.'

'And their bodies were found ripped to bits, yes?'

'Well, yes,' Jimm said, as if that should be obvious.

'Great, brilliant! Well, not for them obviously,' the Doctor admitted. 'But that creature, Kevin. He *is* the Black Shadow. Or *a* Black Shadow. Probably there are lots of them.'

'How's that work, then?' Rose wondered.

'Oh, I dunno. He said something about how the mark on the paper somehow resonates in the Black Dimension where they live and move and have their being. It draws them. It's like a contract which they have to fulfil for their master.'

'Their master?' Bobb was shaking his head. 'I must confess you're losing me now. How does one become master of such a creature?'

'Some artefact in this dimension, this universe, which acts as a link between the master and servant. If the servant, the monster, doesn't fulfil its contract then somehow that link destroys it, or…' He paused mid-stride and snapped his fingers. 'Kevin talked about suffering and torment, maybe that's it.'

'That's what?' Jimm asked.

'Maybe Kevin and his mates don't like the Black Dimension. They get out when they can, as often as they can. Some sort of dimensional bridge that allows that, maybe keyed to their bioprint or whatever they have instead of DNA.'

'So he's like Aladdin's genie?' Rose said. 'Whoever has this bridge thing can, like, rub the lamp and they can come out. But they have to do as they're told or they get stuffed back in and they're stuck there.'

'Exactly so.' The Doctor tapped his teeth with his finger. 'Might even be the origin of the myth, you never know.'

'And he doesn't like it, does he?' Rose realised. 'That's why… Kevin keeps apologising. He's sorry he has to do it, but he does have to do it.'

'And he let me off on a rather dubious technicality,' the Doctor agreed.

'So how does this help?' Jimm asked.

The Doctor had walked quickly over to the photograph by the door. 'This shape, this shadow at the edge of the picture.'

'It's one of those creatures, isn't it?' Rose said.

'More than that. I think it's actually Kevin. I think it's the same creature that Glint had at his beck and call who is killing people and terrorising Starfall. Well, terrorising me anyway.'

'But,' Jimm said, struggling to work it all out, 'wouldn't that mean that someone has the bottle, the bridge you talked about?'

'Yeah.'

'That used to belong to Glint.'

'Yeah.'

'And they know how to use it.'

'Yeah.'

'And they're calling this monster up to kill people, using some old artefact or relic of Glint's.'

'Yeah.'

'But who could it be?' Rose said. 'Must be someone who knows about Glint and has some of his old stuff.'

The Doctor, Rose and Jimm all turned slowly to look in the same direction.

'Don't look at me,' said Bobb.

The Doctor was walking across the room, his face set in stone. He leaned forward to look Bobb straight in the eye from point-blank range. 'You could have slipped the Black Shadow into my pocket at any time,' he said, and his voice was low and dark. 'What's my name?'

'I beg your pardon?'

'What's my name?' the Doctor thundered.

'I don't know,' Bobb shouted back at him. 'As far as I'm aware you're just the Doctor. You've never told me your name.'

The Doctor grinned and slapped Bobb on the shoulder. 'That's right, I never did. Good, well, I'm glad that's settled.'

'So, where's that leave us, then?' Rose asked after an awkward pause, during which the Doctor slumped into an armchair.

'Well, we're not going to sort things out by sitting around here nattering,' the Doctor said.

'And the alternative is?' asked Bobb.

The Doctor blew out a long, heavy breath. 'I think,' he said slowly, 'that our best course of action right now is…' He paused to click his tongue thoughtfully.

'Yes?' Rose prompted.

'Is to go and have a look at Glint's ship.'

'But we don't know where it is,' Jimm pointed out.

'Oh yes, we do,' the Doctor said. 'It won't be hard to find.'

'It sounds crazy to me,' Bobb said when the Doctor had finished. 'And anyway, I don't have the money to hire a ship and a crew to get you there.'

'Really?' The Doctor sounded surprised. 'Are you sure?'

'What do you think?'

'Look, have I got this right?' Rose asked. 'You can actually work out where this Glint bloke's ship is from the way its engines worked or something?'

'Pretty much,' the Doctor agreed. 'Every ship's engines give out a slightly different emission pattern. The engineers call it the engine's signature because it's unique to that ship.'

'And you just need to have something, or rather several somethings, that have been on Glint's ship for a long time. Yes?'

'That's right.'

'And from these things you can detect this signature thing?'

The Doctor nodded. 'Like I said, every nucleo-burn engine has a different signature, and there will be a residue, just a touch of it. But enough to take a reading hopefully.'

'And then you can detect the engine from that?'

'There are a few ifs,' the Doctor admitted. 'But yes.'

'Ifs?'

'Yes,' Bobb put in, ticking them off on his fingers. 'Like, *if* he can find some things that have definitely been on Glint's ship, and *if* he can detect the signature, and *if* it's the right signature, not one from some other ship altogether. And *if* he manages all that, then he can trace the ship *if* the engine's still warm and resonating after fifty years, and *if* he can get close enough so it's in range.'

'That's what I said,' the Doctor agreed with a winning smile. '*If* I can get us a ship and crew.'

'Why don't we get this signature thing sorted first?' Rose asked. 'Then we have something to bargain with.'

'The promise of a share in Glint's treasure!' Jimm said. 'Lots of captains would sail for that.'

'Good thought,' the Doctor said. 'But…'

'Oh, there's buts as well as ifs now?' Rose said. 'Only asking.'

'But,' the Doctor went on, 'I need some pretty specialist equipment to get a reading.'

Now Rose saw the full extent of the 'but'. '*But* it won't work, right? Not until we get it away from the zeg.'

'Right. And to do that, we need funding for a ship.'

'And I don't know who'll have the money and the inclination to stump up funding on the strength of that mad scheme,' Bobb said with a finality that dampened what was left of Rose's optimism.

'I do,' said Jimm. 'You could ask Drel McCavity. He's got loads of money, and he's been after Glint's treasure, and he has artefacts, and he'd do it, I'm sure.'

'Really?' Rose said.

And she could tell from the Doctor's smile, Jimm's excitement and Bobb's look of dour resignation that the boy was probably right.

Jimm had claimed to know a short cut to Drel McCavity's house and before long he and the Doctor and Rose were walking along the driveway. The bodyguards remembered the Doctor and snapped to attention as he greeted them. One of them went to announce the arrival of the inspector of the Watch.

McCavity seemed surprised to see the Doctor again so soon, and even more surprised to meet Rose. The Doctor introduced her as 'Miss Taylor' and she glared at him. Jimm, of course, McCavity already knew. McCavity led them into the study.

'Who's the woman in all the pictures?' Rose whispered.

'Guess,' the Doctor replied quietly.

'Oh. Yeah, right.'

'So, how can I help you?' McCavity asked. He listened with a mixture of incredulity and mounting excitement as the Doctor explained.

'And how would you rate your chances of success?' he asked when the Doctor was done.

'To be honest? Fair to middling.'

McCavity nodded. His mouth was working for a few moments, as if he was muttering to himself, before he spoke out loud. 'Very well. I'm glad to hear you're not completely gung-ho but retain some sense of realism. But tell me, where are you looking? I assume you don't intend traipsing halfway across the galaxy on a fool's errand.'

'Of course not.' The Doctor leaned forward. 'I believe that Glint *was* heading this way. I believe, for various reasons I can't divulge right now, that his ship ran into the zeg and he was stranded. Fifty years ago it wasn't properly mapped or charted and he got caught. Simple as that. He's there somewhere, in among the hundreds of other ships that have conked out over the years. He's in the Outreaches.'

'Which was always possible,' McCavity said slowly. 'Always likely, in fact. But without this engine signature you think you can provide, it would be like looking for a single drop in an ocean.' He smiled thinly. 'Yes, Doctor, I like it.'

'You'll fund the expedition, then?' Jimm wanted to know.

'With certain conditions.'

'Which are?' Rose asked.

'I'm not prepared to invest a large amount. As much as is necessary, but no more.'

'Fair enough,' the Doctor said.

'So we are talking about a small ship. Just you and the crew. The cheapest crew you can sensibly find. Weight will be an issue, as it always is, so we keep it small and light.'

'Agreed,' the Doctor said. 'I do have some equipment I need to bring of course.' He smiled at Rose. 'I keep it locked up safely in a big blue box.'

And at that moment, Rose saw the Doctor's plan. Maybe he really could detect some engine signature and track down Glint's ship. But what he really wanted to do, what this was really all about, was getting the TARDIS to the edge of the zeg zone so it started working again. Finding Glint, if it ever happened, would be a bonus, not the main event. They'd needed a ship, and now it seemed they had one.

'There is just one other condition,' McCavity was saying. 'I'm coming with you.'

Jimm went skipping on ahead as they walked back towards the docks, so Rose was able to talk to the Doctor.

'Weird guy,' Rose said. 'Why's he keep muttering under his breath?'

'He's talking to his wife,' the Doctor said as if that was obvious.

'But his wife's left him.' Rose shook her head. 'Yeah, right. But he still talks to her.'

'That's about it.'

'Is he mad or what?'

'A bit north by north-west maybe.'

'Thought that was an old film,' Rose said. 'So, can you really find Glint's ship?'

'Oh yeah, I think so. But not quite in the way I said.'

'How, then?'

'With this.' He held up what looked like dark fluff. 'I really do need a signature from something that has spent a lot of time on the ship, and which hasn't spent much time on another ship since.'

'And what is that, exactly?'

'It's a tuft of fur I pulled out of Kevin's arm when he was waving me about above his head.'

'Oh, nice.'

'And I'm pretty sure that he's spent a lot of time on Glint's ship one way and another. So I can try to get a signature from this, and see if it matches signatures from a few other Glint artefacts by way of confirmation. If it does, then we know we're on to a winner.'

'And if it doesn't?'

'We're stuffed and we leave in the TARDIS.'

'And this all assumes that the ship really is in these Outreaches or wherever.'

'Must be somewhere nearby. Kevin's able to dimension jump in and out of reality, but that's a pretty short-range process the way he probably does it. So I'm betting that his master, whoever that is, summoned him from his previous home, which I'm hoping was the ship.'

'So, lots more ifs and buts.'

'Just a few.'

'And what's with the Miss Taylor stuff?'

'Just insurance. Lots of people know you're called Rose, but if we get them thinking you're Rose Taylor, that may help.'

'Why?'

'Because Kevin let me off the hook when he found out he'd got my name wrong.'

That made sense, Rose decided. 'Insurance? But,' she pointed out, 'Kevin fancies me.'

'Then let's hope he doesn't love you to death. Hey, Jimm!' the Doctor called to the boy scampering on ahead. 'Fancy a quick sherbert at the Spyglass? We'll put it on Bobb's tab.'

'Oh, it's nice just to chill for a bit and not feel like I'm on duty or something,' Rose said. She had risked a small tankard of grog and was pleasantly surprised to find it tasted more like ginger beer than real ale.

'Been busy, then?' Silver Sally asked, handing the Doctor his own tankard of grog.

'Always busy,' the Doctor told her. 'Always on the case.'

'We're going to find Glint's treasure,' Jimm said.

'Keep your voice down,' Rose warned.

But Sally was laughing. Steam puffed out from her joints in sympathy. 'You and everyone else who comes in here,' she said.

'No, really,' Jimm insisted. 'The Doctor's got it all sorted.'

'Well, not quite all,' he admitted modestly.

'Still a few ifs and buts,' Rose said, but she had caught the Doctor's tone and realised that there was a reason he had brought them to the inn and it wasn't just for a drink. 'So why are we here really?'

'Pleasant company,' he said. 'Nice drinkies. Good to see Sally again. And this is just the place, I think, to find a cheap crew.'

Sally stared at him. 'Are you serious? I mean, seriously serious?'

'Oh yes.'

'And you need a crew?'

'Cheaper the better. So long as they know their stuff. No shirkers, no lurkers and no ground-lubbers allowed.'

'I'll get you a crew,' Sally said.

'Really?' The Doctor was beaming. 'Well, of course, working here you must have contacts.'

'A cheap crew and a good cook.'

The Doctor's eyes narrowed.

'Here we go again,' Rose said. 'Just one condition, right?'

'Actually, two,' Sally told them. 'Crew'll have to be robotic, that's the cheapest and the best you'll get.'

'How appropriate,' the Doctor murmured.

'And if we find anything, they won't hassle for a huge cut or set you adrift in a space lane full of hungry krarks.'

'If *we* find anything?' the Doctor queried.

'Told you,' Rose said.

The human half of Silver Sally's face was smiling. 'Gets me out of this dump, and like I said, you'll need a good cook. Hey, let's go find some treasure!'

'I'll drink to that,' Rose said. And she did.

FIVE

It just wasn't fair. Jimm was shouting at Bobb in a blazing fury and getting nowhere. 'Who suggested asking McCavity?' he stormed. 'I did! It was my idea. I want to go. I have a right to go.'

'You don't,' Bobb said calmly and quietly. 'And you're not going, I tell you.'

His calm response just made it seem worse. 'You never let me do anything,' Jimm shouted back. His eyes were so full of tears that he could hardly see. But he didn't want to cry in front of Rose and the Doctor. 'You won't even let me go to the docks and watch the ships leaving or unloading, and now…' He broke off in a near sob.

'You're not going, and that's final. You're too young, too inexperienced.'

'How will I get experience if I never *do* anything?'

'I'm not sure this would be the best trip to get experience on,' the Doctor said, and his words were as calm and quiet and unwelcome as Uncle Bobb's.

'They're right,' Rose told him gently. She put an arm round his shoulder and he shrugged it off. 'It could be dangerous. And we'll tell you what we find...' She broke off, as if she'd said something she shouldn't. 'Well, you'll soon know if we find Glint's ship and treasure and everything, won't you?'

'Maybe next time,' the Doctor said. 'When we know where we're going. Maybe then.'

'I hate you!' Jimm hissed. 'All of you. You're all as bad as each other. You all want me to stay on Starfall all my life and never do anything or go anywhere. I hate it and I hate you. If you won't help me get into space, I'll find someone who will!' And he ran from the room.

'He'll be all right,' Bobb said when Jimm had gone. 'Let him sulk and cool his heels for a bit.'

'I appreciate your point of view,' the Doctor said. 'But I did think you'd bring him with you.'

Bobb laughed. 'Oh, I'm not coming,' he said. 'You find Glint's treasure, you tell me all about it. But I'm too old, just as Jimm's too young, to go gallivanting about across the Outreaches hunting for lost ships and trying to avoid the krarks. Good luck to you, but no thanks.'

'Oh.' The Doctor sounded genuinely disappointed. 'Well, never mind.'

'I'd have thought it was right up your street,' Rose said. 'What with all your collection and interest and everything.'

'Some things are best left as legends,' Bobb told her. 'Sometimes it's better to dream than to know for sure. And like I said, I'm too old to go chasing dreams anyway.'

'But if we find this Resurrection Casket thing...'

Bobb was shaking his head. 'I don't know about McCavity, but I'm getting close to the end of my life and that's fine by me. Jimm'll be old enough to look after himself soon, and to be honest it's him I live for. Once he no longer needs me, then I'll happily shuffle off. Who wants to live for ever?'

'Well,' the Doctor said. 'Quite.'

'Say goodbye to Jimm for us, won't you?' Rose said.

'I will. And you'll be able to tell him all about it when you get back. Like you promised.'

Rose glanced at the Doctor, then forced a smile. 'Yeah,' she said. 'Course we will.'

The ship was called *Venture* and was smaller than most of the others at the docks. But it still stood as high as an office block, towering above Rose and the Doctor as they stood looking up at it. Steam was rolling down its oily sides and the whole structure seemed to shiver in its berth.

A massive steam-driven crane had swung the TARDIS across and the Doctor had given instructions for it to be stored somewhere out of the way. After a degree of haggling it was agreed to put it in the forward escape pod.

'The ceilings are fairly low on most of the ship,' the Doctor explained. 'And I really don't want the poor girl lying on her side.'

'Yeah, poor thing,' Rose said, lacing her voice with sarcasm.

'Because,' the Doctor said, pretending he hadn't heard, 'it would make it so difficult for you to climb in and out.'

'Thanks. So there are two escape pods – is it that safe, then?'

'Safe as houses. Twice as safe with two escape pods,' the Doctor said. 'Safe as two houses.'

McCavity joined them, and together they watched as his own belongings were loaded. He had brought a small suitcase, a large, uniformed minder, and a very large wooden trunk that Rose remembered seeing in his study.

'What's in there?' she asked, amused. 'Brought some treasure of your own?'

'It has sentimental value,' he said. 'Doesn't it, my dear?' he added, just loud enough for Rose to hear him this time.

'Not Glint's old space chest, then?' the Doctor asked.

'I'm afraid it isn't, no. It's mine. A few bits and pieces for the journey.'

'Just like the old days, when everyone had a space chest to keep his tack and tucker,' the Doctor said. 'Aha!' he added, sounding like a pantomime pirate.

'Yes,' McCavity agreed quietly. 'Just like the old days.'

And Rose wasn't sure if he was talking to them or to his long-lost wife.

'Time to board, me hearties,' the Doctor announced. 'Look lively, lads.' He led the way to the metal steps that rose up from the quay to the entrance hatchway in the side of the ship. McCavity's bodyguard gestured for the Doctor to go first.

'Oh yes,' the Doctor told Rose as they ascended. 'I remember him as if it were yesterday, as he came plodding to the inn door, his space chest following behind him in a steam barrow…'

'I bet you do,' she laughed.

The take-off was like nothing Rose had ever experienced before. When the ground crew strapped her into the flight seat and harnessed the restraining straps, she thought they were just being mean and taking the mickey, they pulled them so tight. Then one of the men standing on the level above where Rose was sitting put his foot on her shoulder and wrenched the strap tighter still.

She gasped in pain, but seeing the Doctor and McCavity and McCavity's bodyguard undergoing the same treatment further along, she said nothing. Presumably Silver Sally and the three oily, steaming robots she had brought with her were getting similar attention in the aft quarters.

The hatches were closed and sealed, and the vibration that ran through the ship increased. Before long the whole structure was shaking. Rose tried to call to the Doctor, but her voice was lost in the hiss and roar of steam, and she bit her tongue she was shaking so much.

With a final earthquaking heave, she felt herself pressed down into the seat. There was an observation porthole alongside her, but all she could see was smoke. Then for a moment it parted, and Rose caught a glimpse of the world below dropping rapidly away.

'Why do we need these straps so tight?' she said through gritted teeth as she was pressed still further into the chair. But even she didn't hear her own voice.

Then the pressure eased off as they rose through the narrow band of atmosphere and Rose found out. It was only a slight change, but it slammed her so hard against the straps she felt her whole body was going to be sliced into bits. 'Who needs Kevin and his claws?' she muttered into the furious noise.

Gently, slowly, when Rose was almost fainting and feeling that if she survived she'd surely hurl her lunch across the room, the pressure eased again. If she was sick, she wondered, would it just float round the ship? The thought made her feel worse and she clamped her mouth tight shut.

In fact, there was gravity, which must make things much easier.

'So how come they have fake gravity when there's no electronics or technology more advanced than the seat belts?' she asked the Doctor when she felt it was safe to open her mouth again.

'Gyroscopes,' he said, immediately warming to the subject. 'Very clever. There's a big one right underneath us now. That's why even little ships are so heavy and need all that steam to take off. Well, that and the water. No smoke without fire, no steam without water. They could shoot us out of a huge cannon, I suppose, but where's the fun in that?' He didn't wait for Rose's reply, which was just as well as she didn't have one. 'Y'know how the gyroscope you got for your birthday when you were seven – or was it eight…? Never mind – anyway, you know how when it spins round it can balance on top of that little model of the Eiffel Tower? Well, that's the same sort of idea. The whole ship is like the ring round that gyroscope and we're all perched on top of the Eiffel Tower. I used to wonder why it was always the Eiffel Tower they used, but then it struck me.'

'Oh?' Rose said. It was all she had time for before he was off again.

'You see, if they used the Leaning Tower of Pisa, kids would miss the point. They'd be forever trying to stand it up without realising it's actually made that way.'

'Fancy that,' Rose said. 'How long's this trip going to take, then?'

The Doctor shrugged. 'Not long.' He inspected his nails. 'Probably just a week or two.' Then he covered his ears.

* * *

There were three robots running the ship. Silver Sally introduced Rose to them as if they were old friends. All three were very different, though all were of course powered by steam. Like Sally's prosthetic half, their metal bodies were forever hissing and puffing. They didn't speak, but there seemed to be a convention that one puff of steam from the head meant 'yes' and two meant 'no'. As a way of communicating it seemed to work, but anything more than simple instructions quickly turned into a long-winded game of Twenty Questions as hosted by George Stephenson.

The first time Rose met Kenny was when Sally was cooking some sort of stir-fry in the narrow galley kitchen, and Rose was trying to be helpful while getting in the way a lot. Kenny was the tallest and thinnest of the robots. His body was made up of tarnished metal plates riveted in place, with a bulbous head sitting precariously on top of a thin neck. Steam hissed out from the joints when he moved, and his face was a crude approximation. Dark holes for eyes, no hint of a nose, and a wide rectangle covered with mesh for a mouth. He was, Sally explained, responsible for the general maintenance of the ship.

'Like plumbing?' Rose asked. She meant it as a joke, but it turned out that was actually a large part of Kenny's job.

'There's over seven miles of pipes,' Sally told her. 'And this ship's a small one. Only four boilers, but then the steam gets piped through the infrastructure.

And the water has to get from the central reservoirs to the boilers in the first place. You can imagine the mess if a pipe bursts.'

'Does that happen often?' Rose asked.

A single puff of white steam blew out from Kenny's mouth.

'Space is very cold, remember,' Sally said. 'The water pipes freeze and split if they're not steamed regularly. But as well as the plumbing there's the whole integrity of the hull to think about. Basically it's just plates of metal hammered and riveted together. The slightest leak and there goes our oxygen. That's assuming the whole ship doesn't get ripped open by the decompression.'

'Too much detail,' Rose told her. 'Thanks, I get the idea. So, keep up the good work, Kenny.'

Kenny left to go about his duties, and was soon replaced in the galley by the smaller humanoid figure of King. This robot sparkled as if it was covered in sequins. It moved almost gracefully, though on tree-trunk-wide legs, and had a habit of answering questions with a double puff of steam that sounded as if it was saying, 'Uh-huh.'

King, Sally said, was responsible for navigation and piloting. It was King who actually flew the ship. Since it just continued in a straight line unless and until there was any need for a course correction or a change of speed, this meant that King seemed to have a lot of time to himself. Like the other two robots, he obviously knew Sally very well and seemed to prefer her company to that of any of the other passengers.

Finally, there was Jonesy. Sally took Rose down to the engine rooms to meet him, as Jonesy ran the boilers. He kept them constantly fuelled and hot so that there was never a shortage of steam. It seemed to be pretty much a full-time job, though Sally said the other robots came and helped and gave him some time off when they could.

Perhaps because of where he worked, or perhaps because he simply wasn't very well put together, Jonesy seemed to be forever stained with oil and soot. His plastic 'face' was smudged across like a chimney sweep's, and he seemed to be leaking dark fluid from every joint. When he moved, he hissed and wheezed and creaked as if he was about to seize up or fall apart. Or possibly both.

They were on the way back up to the galley from the main engine room when the ship suddenly shuddered. A metallic clang echoed down the stairwell, and Rose grabbed at the rail to stop herself from being thrown to the floor. Sally's tiny engines whirred and hissed and protested as she struggled to keep her balance.

'What was that?' Rose gasped.

'I don't know. No sign of decompression. Collision maybe.'

'We hit something?'

They started cautiously back up the stairs. 'Or something hit us,' Sally said. 'Let's take a look.'

At the top of the stairs was an observation panel – a large porthole in the side of the ship. A thick, circular glass window fused into the metal of the ship's hull, looking out into the oily blackness of space. The view was misty, like peering through clouds, from the steam of the ship's exhaust.

'Can't see anything,' Rose said.

Then she gave a cry of surprise and took a step backwards as a dark shape hurled itself towards her. A huge mouth that seemed to be all pointed teeth slammed into the glass, smearing saliva across the view.

'What is that?' Rose demanded, unable to look away as the creature backed off. It turned slowly, elegantly, its fish-like body quivering as it manoeuvred.

'It's a krark,' Sally said. 'The panel should be strong enough to keep it out. But it's seen you and thinks you're lunch.'

Sure enough, the creature hurled itself at the glass again. Rose flinched, even though she knew there was thick glass between them. The krark looked about the size of a shark, similar in shape except it had no fins and its tail was a sharp point. Tiny round holes dotted its side and Rose could see them opening and closing like mouths.

'That's how it moves,' Sally said, seeing what Rose was looking at. 'The krark can store an immense amount of oxygen-rich gas. It can suck it out of tiny pockets, or the upper atmosphere of planets and moons. It compresses it, so it can go for months without a fresh supply. It blows out tiny amounts under enormous pressure through those holes so it can move.'

'Quick, aren't they?' Rose said as the krark turned for another attack.

'Deadly. Rip you apart as soon as look at you. Anything to get the air from your lungs, or the steam from inside this ship. Any gas will do – if they can't breathe it they can still use it.'

'The same way this ship uses steam,' Rose realised.

'Exactly. Anyway, it'll get bored soon and look for easier pickings elsewhere.'

'It can't get in, can it?' Rose asked nervously as they reached the galley.

'Course not,' Sally assured her. 'Occasionally they get lucky and you hear of a ship that didn't bother having its hull plates checked and then got ripped to pieces by a shoal of krarks. But so long as everything's riveted down you're OK.'

'And that's Kenny's job, right? Let's hope he's good at it.'

'He's the best,' Sally said simply.

'You've known him a long time?'

Sally shrugged, steam misting out from her left-shoulder joints. 'Known them all for a while, I suppose.'

'I didn't see many robots on Starfall,' Rose said.

'So?'

Rose shrugged. 'I was just saying.'

'The robots get the more difficult and dangerous jobs – in the docks or down the mines. Not as efficient as on other planets of course, because they need to keep topping up with water and the steam needs to vent.'

'They get time off?' Rose wondered. 'Get to down a few pints of H_2O?'

'It's a bit like that actually. They all have personality and character traits laid in. Bit clunky on a steam-based motherboard but it's all there. So yeah, they socialise, sort of. Get downtime. Have arguments about hours and rates of pay, though they're programmed to believe that their masters know best of course. Some hope to get a placement on one of the ships.'

'You know a lot about ships too,' Rose pointed out.

Half of Sally's face frowned. 'What do you mean?'

'Sorry, I don't mean anything. You know more than me and that's a fact.'

The half-frown became a half-smile. 'Sorry, didn't mean to snap at you like a krark. It's just that people assume that I've always worked at the Spyglass and I haven't, you know. I'm older than I look. I've worked my time on the ships as well.'

Rose nodded. 'And you miss it,' she realised. 'You're glad to be back out here, aren't you?'

'Nothing else like it,' Sally said. 'It's what I was made for.'

It was a strange way of putting it, and Rose wondered if Sally was being sarcastic. 'Like Jimm,' she joked. 'He was so disappointed.'

'Yes,' Sally said.

Over the last few days, Rose had come to admire as well as like Sally. She admired the way the girl coped with her disabilities – how she managed and seemed always to be cheerful and positive and optimistic despite having lost half her body, despite having frequently to open up parts of her artificial side and top up with water...

Rose never asked how it happened; an accident she assumed. Sally never offered to speak about it, and Rose took that as another indication that the girl had accepted and overcome her ordeal, whatever it was.

More than anything, Rose felt guilty for feeling sorry for her. Sally didn't need or want her sympathy, Rose was sure. More than anything, she must want to be seen and treated just like anyone else.

'Look,' Sally was saying, 'I need to sort out some food.'

'Can I help?'

'Thanks, but it's a bit cramped in here. I'll be quicker left to it, I think. But it's good to have company. I'll see you soon, all right?'

When she wasn't with Silver Sally, Rose spent most of her time in the main living quarters. Here, the Doctor and Drel McCavity had papered the metal walls with maps and star charts. Every so often, King would update the red line that showed their progress, inching it slowly closer to the Outreaches.

McCavity's bodyguard was pressed into service as a general dogsbody, fetching food from Sally in the kitchen and chasing King for more and more frequent – and more and more slight – updates. His name, Rose discovered in a few moments of rare communication, was Dugg.

'I'm only doing this job until I write my bestselling holo-book,' he told Rose.

'Have you written much of it?' she asked. 'What's it about?'

Dugg grunted something about planning and romantic comedy and needing an agent and interested publishers. Neither of them spoke of it again, but Rose noticed he carried a small notebook in his pocket and was often jotting in it.

Every day the Doctor went to the TARDIS, and every day Rose went with him. Every day they stood in front of it, and the Doctor held up his key and it was just an ordinary key that didn't glow or anything. And when he put it in the lock, nothing happened – it wouldn't turn. And every day the Doctor sighed and said quietly, 'Maybe tomorrow, then. Tomorrow will be good. I like tomorrow.'

Rose reckoned it would be four days before he got bored with it. In fact, it was three.

'Right,' he announced that third day as the TARDIS

again refused to open. 'That's it. I'm going to sort this out.' He squared his shoulders, wobbled his head as if to ease a stiff neck and set off towards the engine rooms.

'What are you going to do?' Rose called, hurrying after him.

He was pulling off his coat and rolling up his sleeves. 'Going to sort it out. Going to improve their inefficient, slow, wasteful, rubbish engines and get us there in a day instead of a week. I mean, have you seen how they pump the steam? No real compressor, no idea about condensing, a centrifugal governor that's out of the Ark – and I mean *Noah's* Ark – and as for stoking the boilers, well…'

'Right,' Rose said, letting him stride off purposefully into the distance. 'Kicking bottom, then. You show 'em.'

In fact it took more than a day for the Doctor to 'recalibrate the centrifugal governors and enhance the engines', whatever that meant. But two days later, the TARDIS unlocked. The systems inside seemed to be largely powered down, though the lights were working weakly and without the constant flickering, and the Doctor fussed and worried at the main console.

'Can we leave?' Rose asked.

'Wouldn't recommend it. Might cut out in mid-dematerialisation and scatter bits of us through time and space.'

'Nasty.'

'To say the least. Won't be long, though. As the influence of the zeg fades and diminishes, so more and more of the TARDIS is working again. Maybe tomorrow.' He grinned, face almost satanic in the gloom. 'Should be able to track down the elusive Mr Glint, though.' He brandished the tuft of Kevin's fur. 'Let me get a couple of things from Mr McCavity that Bobb was kind enough to supply and we can draw ourselves a treasure map.'

'Terrific. Be nice to find some treasure before we just slip off in our old TARDIS, now it's not dying any more.'

'Old TARDISes never die,' the Doctor told her as they went back out into the escape pod. 'They simply fade away.'

'Is this going to be boring?' Rose wondered. 'This getting a signature thing and mapping the position and everything?'

'Boring?' He paused briefly to consider the question. 'Excruciatingly,' he decided, rubbing his hands together. 'I'm looking forward to it.'

'Me too,' Rose said. 'How about you sort it all out and I'll see you later?'

She thought she'd find Sally to give her a progress report. The girl would be excited, Rose knew, at the prospect of finally finding Glint's ship and she was looking forward to being the bringer of good news. Rose liked Sally a lot, and of course she assumed that

Sally felt the same about her.

So discovering the truth was a shock.

There was a small mess hall off the galley. Since the passengers ate in the main living quarters, Sally used it for storage and the cupboards were filled with dried and vacuum-packed food and drink.

Rose saw King walking through the mess hall to the galley as she entered. The robot did not seem to have seen her, and Rose was about to call out when she heard Sally's voice from inside the galley.

'Oh, it's you,' Sally said. Her voice sounded more abrupt than usual. 'Thank heavens. I thought it was that stupid girl again. Sometimes I think she's tied to me by rigging rope. Daft bitch.'

Rose stopped mid-step. For a second she wondered who Sally could be talking about. Then her blood froze cold and her mouth was suddenly dry.

'Where are the others?' Sally was asking. 'With these engine improvements McCavity thinks the Doctor will be able to get his equipment working and give us a reading soon.'

Rose tiptoed towards the galley door, still hoping that she had misheard or misunderstood.

King was standing with his metal back to the door, so she could not see the robot's face. But she heard him speak – for the first time, she heard him speak.

'Voice returns,' he grated. It was a scraping, rusty sound.

'We're getting to the edge of the zeg. I can feel it too,' Sally replied. 'Soon, Elvis, soon we'll be able to function properly. Oh, how I hate this face,' she snarled suddenly. 'Every time I look in the mirror I see that idiot girl from the Spyglass looking back at me.'

'Others come soon,' King said – but why had Sally called him 'Elvis'?

Behind her, Rose could hear the puff and hiss of the other robots approaching the mess hall. In a few moments they would be here, they would find her. How embarrassing would that be now she knew what Sally really thought of her. But already she was thinking it might be more than just embarrassing.

She was sure of it when King (Elvis?) said, 'Others come now, Salvo.'

Salvo?

She could hear the metallic thump of footsteps from outside.

She could see the robot in the galley turning back towards the mess – towards her.

And she could hear the Doctor's voice in her head, could remember every nuance and inflection and hint of amusement when he had told her about Glint's robot crew, and about Salvo 7-50: 'the fiercest and most vicious pirate of the lot'.

SIX

She had only moments to find somewhere to hide. The room was bare and empty. There was a table against the wall, but no way would Rose be safe just sitting underneath it. Table, chairs, cupboards.

Cupboards. They didn't look very big, but there was nowhere else. The hiss and puff of steam was almost there. Less than moments.

The first cupboard she opened was full of cooking pots and pans, and far too small for Rose to squeeze into even if it had been empty. But the next door she opened, while no larger, gave into a wide cupboard that ran behind several of the small doors. It was almost empty, and she dived inside, scrabbling to pull the door shut behind her, trying desperately not to knock into the plates and mugs that were piled up at one end. She pushed her legs gently along, feeling for the space, and her feet hit something at the end of the cupboard. Something soft but heavy – maybe a pile of tablecloths or towels.

Aware now of just how much – or rather how little – space she had, Rose lay curled and still, trying to angle herself so she could see through the narrow crack between the cupboard door and its frame. It afforded her a view of a slice of the room outside – enough to see Silver Sally and King enter from the galley. Just in time, Rose thought with relief, hardly daring to breathe.

'Elvis is getting his voice back,' Sally was saying. Rose could hear clearly through the ill-fitting door.

'All voices return,' another metallic voice grated.

'That's right, Smithers,' Sally replied. 'And you'll get yours back soon enough, Cannon, now we're near the edge of the zeg. I can feel the power returning to my limbs, and it feels good.'

'You get own face back?' King croaked.

Rose almost gasped – how could that happen?

'Sadly not,' Sally was saying. 'But after over a year, I'm getting used to it. Why did Glint have to head into this wilderness? Having to repair myself with organic parts is a real pain, I can tell you. Have you any idea how much of a drain on the systems it is pumping blood round?'

In her cupboard, Rose swallowed and closed her eyes as she listened to the girl's words.

'What a design,' Sally went on. 'It's a wonder they work at all, you know. Maybe I can get a decent repair job done when this is over. Glint used to say he saw the faces of the people he'd killed when he slept. I see *her* face every day.'

'Murder and theft,' King said. Despite the level electronic voice, he somehow sounded amused.

But in the dark cupboard, Rose was gagging at the thought of robot Sally repairing herself with bits of people she had killed. How gross was that? She thought for a moment about who the real Sally might have been. What life had she had? What had been her ambitions and dreams?

But Sally – or rather robot Salvo 7-50 – was speaking again: 'All that time on Starfall, it had better be worth it.'

'Artefacts turn up,' the voice that Sally had called 'Smithers' said.

'You're right. Once bits of Glint's treasure started to turn up, we had to act. Someone has found it, or part of it. And I want what's rightfully ours. If the Doctor really can find Glint's ship, then we kill them all and we're back in business, my metal friends.'

'Soon now,' Smithers agreed. 'Power returning. Systems online soon. Then steam no more.'

'That's right. The sooner we can dump this excess weight and antiquated technology, the better.'

Rose shuddered. The steam technology was just a makeshift solution to the lack of technology in the zeg. Who knew how dangerous and powerful these robots must really be? Inadvertently, without even realising she was doing it, she repositioned herself slightly. Her foot pushed at the soft weight at the end of the cupboard and it shifted.

There was a thump as something moved or fell.

Silence in the room outside.

Then: 'What was that?' Smithers's scraping voice demanded.

'I don't know… Unless.'

Through the crack in the door, Rose could see Sally approaching the cupboards. She stopped right outside the door, looking, it seemed, directly at Rose.

'Must have been our young friend in the cupboard,' Sally said.

And she pulled open the cupboard door.

'I can assure you that this came from Glint's treasure,' McCavity told the Doctor. 'Can't we, darling?' he murmured as he took a chain from round his neck. Hanging from it was a gold medallion. He hesitated a moment, then handed it to the Doctor.

'How do you know that?' the Doctor asked.

The medallion was plain – no engraving or inscription. Just flat, polished gold. It was heavy, and it fitted neatly into the palm of the Doctor's hand. McCavity seemed unable to take his eyes from it.

'Just accept that I do.'

'Well, if you're sure. But, I mean, it has been known for you to buy dud Glint stuff assuming it's real. Hasn't it? No offence.'

Offence or not, Dugg's eyes narrowed as he waited for his master's reaction.

But McCavity smiled thinly. 'It's genuine,' he said. 'I

know.' Again, his voice dropped to barely a murmur: 'Don't I, Larissa, my darling?'

The Doctor smiled back. 'All right, then. That gives us two genuine artefacts.' He pulled the tuft of fur from his coat pocket and put it down on the table next to the medallion. 'Don't ask,' he said without looking up. 'Now, assuming we get the same signature reading from both of these, then each confirms the other.'

'And if they are different?'

'Then we have to decide which, if either, to trust and scan for.'

'How long will it take before you know?'

The Doctor's sonic screwdriver was in his hand. He squeezed it experimentally and was rewarded with a pale blue glow from the end. He grinned massively. 'Could be as long as a minute.'

'They are so funny,' Sally said. 'Moving when they don't intend to. Sometimes they don't even know about it. Taking this ship will be a doddle when the time comes.'

'Pity the others not see it,' Smithers ground out.

'Dusty, Stubbs and Octo,' Sally said sadly as she closed the cupboard door again, cutting off the view of the still figure curled inside. 'Yes. But it was quick, at least. Thank goodness they got the crusher, not the furnace. You would have been next, Elvis, if I hadn't managed to get free.'

'No more crushing,' Elvis said.

'And we do the burning,' Smithers added. 'Burn bodies, make steam.'

'What a good idea,' Sally agreed. 'But until we know where the *Buccaneer* is moored, we play along. You three are good little robots helping run the ship, not dastardly pirates out to murder the crew. Got it? Good. Back to your duties, then. I'll let you know when the time comes, but it won't be long now.'

'Soon,' Elvis agreed. Rose could not be sure, but she thought his voice sounded stronger, less of a rasp, more confident and assured.

Rose's heart had skipped a beat when Sally had approached the cupboard. She had almost cried out when Sally opened the door – the door further along, close to Rose's feet – and looked in at whatever was lying soft and heavy at the end of the cupboard. She held her breath until Sally closed the door again, desperate to make no noise. She waited until she was sure the robots had gone, then Rose carefully climbed out of the cupboard.

Slowly, nervously, Rose went to the cupboard door. She took hold of the handle and, full of apprehension at what she might see, she pulled it open. Just as Sally had.

And just like Sally, she saw what was inside. It was a body – still, lifeless, curled into a ball. It was Jimm.

She gasped out loud, then pushed the door closed again quickly as she heard a sound from the galley. Back to work, Sally had said – and she worked in the galley. She was still here.

Sally was wiping her hands on a tea towel as she came in. Her face was the familiar half-smile, but now Rose could see that it did not reach the eye. The human eye. The human eye that was not hers.

'Hello,' Sally said. 'I didn't hear you come in.'

Rose took a step backwards. 'I... I can't stop. Just wondered how dinner was coming along.'

'Fine,' Sally said. But she wasn't looking at Rose now. She was staring through someone else's eyes at the line of cupboards behind. Where Rose realised, her stomach sinking, one of the doors was still open. Half-smile became half-frown.

'Well, see you, then,' Rose said. It was all she could do to walk not run from the room, expecting any moment to feel a metal hand clamp down on her shoulder.

As she finally broke into a run, Rose thought about Jimm. She could hardly bear to leave him, but there was nothing she could do. Sally would kill her if she went back – Rose had seen it in the eye she now had.

But Jimm was alive – he had to be. Sally had thought he'd moved, had told the other robots that it was an involuntary reflex of some sort. But how had he ever got there?

Then she realised. 'If you won't help me get into space, I'll find someone who will!' Jimm had said – and he had gone to Silver Sally. His friend. Or so he thought. And now he was drugged or doped or knocked out and bundled into a cupboard. He must have been in there for days – maybe even suffered the pain and trauma of the take-off just lying in a cupboard as the g-force crushed the breath out of him.

She wiped the tears from her cheek and crashed into the living quarters. The Doctor and McCavity were examining a chart unrolled across the table. Dugg was cleaning his nails with a large, sharp knife.

'Ah, Rose,' the Doctor said, looking up. 'Good news.' He saw her expression as she caught her breath and struggled to speak. 'Just sort of indifferent news?' he ventured. Then he nodded in resignation. 'Bad news.'

'Bad news,' she agreed, lungs protesting. 'Sally isn't Sally. The robots – they're Glint's old crew. She's Salvo whatever number it is.'

'7-50,' McCavity said. 'Are you sure?'

'Are you kidding? I overheard them. I think she knows. And they've got Jimm.'

'Jimm? What's he doing –' The Doctor shook his head and waved his hands. 'No, I don't want to know. I can guess. I dunno, you do things hoping for a quiet life and someone comes and yells in your ear. How thoughtless is that?'

'Dangerous too,' Rose pointed out.

'Dugg,' McCavity said quietly, and the big man put away his knife, sliding it into a holster at his hip. From another holster he produced a blunt-nosed automatic gun.

'Which robots?' the Doctor demanded.

'Sorry?'

'Salvo 7-50 and three others – which ones are they?'

'Does it matter?'

'Can't be Octo,' McCavity said. 'None of them has eight arms.'

'They're disguised,' Rose pointed out. 'Adapted for steam.'

'We'd still have noticed the arms,' the Doctor pointed out. 'I mean, eight – count 'em. So, let's see. King must be Elvis,' he decided. 'That figures.'

'And this is important – why?' Rose said.

'Cannon-K is the one to watch, apart from Salvo,' McCavity was saying. 'Isn't he, my darling?'

'All right, indulge the loonies time,' Rose decided. 'Yeah, one's called Cannon, the King is Elvis, which sounds kind of backwards to me, and Jonesy is Smithers because… Well, just because.'

'Because robots have so little imagination,' the Doctor said. He turned to Dugg. 'Put the gun away and barricade the door.'

Dugg looked to McCavity, who nodded. 'Cannon-K is a battle robot. The gun won't do him any damage.'

'Probably won't worry the others much either,' the Doctor said. 'But I like to look on the bright side.'

'And which bright side is that?' Rose wondered. She helped Dugg and the Doctor push the table across to block the door. 'The side where we're stuck on a ship with homicidal pirate robots?'

'No, not that side.'

'Or the bit where we're trapped in a room with only one door, and we just barricaded ourselves inside?'

The Doctor started piling chairs on top of the table. 'Nor that either.'

'Maybe the fact they have a young kid as a hostage?'

'Don't think that's it, no.'

'Then what?' Rose implored. 'What have we got that could possibly give us an advantage, an edge of any kind? Eh?'

The Doctor stared back at her, hurt. 'You've got *me*,' he said, and his face broke into a huge grin.

'Oh,' said Rose. 'Yeah.' And she grinned back at him.

The grin froze at the sound of hammering from the other side of the door. 'Don't you want your dinner, then?' Sally's voice called from the other side.

'Not hungry,' the Doctor yelled back. 'We'd probably choke on it anyway, am I right?'

Rose could hear her laugh. It had sounded so genuine and uplifting before. Now it sounded false, forced, inhuman. 'Well,' Sally shouted, 'we have a few choices on the menu today.'

'No, no, let me guess,' the Doctor replied. 'For starters we can let you in and you kill us all for the main course. Or we can sit it out in here for a bit while you threaten young Jimm out there. And as a pudding, Cannon-K might decide to blow the door down and you murder us all anyway soon as he gets enough power back. Hardly what I call just desserts.'

'No,' came the reply. 'But killing and murdering are

the house special this week. And we do them *so* well.'

'You don't have anything for people who don't want to be killed, then?' Rose shouted. 'Like a vegetarian option? Pacifist menu?'

'You can't kill us till we've traced the engine signature that will lead us to Glint's ship,' the Doctor called. 'And we need to be further out of the zeg before we can do that.'

There was a short pause. Then Sally replied, 'You're right, I'm afraid. But of course you'll have to die some time, sooner rather than later and horribly rather than quickly if you don't take us to the *Buccaneer*. I'll give you a few minutes if you've not decided. After that, Jimm might find out how sharp the steak knives are, if you get my point. Because he certainly will.'

The Doctor seemed to be spinning in a circle, pinching the bridge of his nose and turning rapidly as he thought. 'Chalkboard,' he decided. 'There's always a chalkboard, you know, with extra choices. And so often you only notice it and see that there's just what you fancied *after* you've already ordered.' He stopped spinning and threw his arms wide as he demanded of them all, 'So, what's on the chalkboard?'

'Raw krark, probably,' Rose told him.

'Is he always like this?' McCavity wanted to know.

'Pretty much,' Rose admitted, adding quietly, 'And you can talk.' Behind him she could see Dugg scribbling furious notes in his little book. Great – big help, she thought.

'If I could get close enough...' McCavity said thoughtfully. 'Do they have pockets?'

'What?' Rose looked to Dugg. 'Is he always like this?'

Dugg quickly put his notebook and pencil away. He frowned in concentration. 'Can't say I've noticed.'

'Krarks!' the Doctor shouted at them from the other side of the room. He was tearing down the charts and maps pinned up on that wall, and then he started on the metal panelling beneath. 'Dugg, give me a hand, will you? I want to get this panel off.'

'Why?' McCavity and Rose both asked at the same time.

'Krarks. Rose, you're brilliant – you know that, don't you? Course you do. Because I bet I keep telling you.' He turned back to help Dugg rip off the wall plate, exposing a cavity filled with pipes. 'Must be a flow valve or pressure shut-off in here somewhere.'

'Can you stop the engines?' Rose said. 'Like, threaten to destroy the ship?'

The Doctor looked at her over his shoulder, expression sympathetic. 'Rose, this is more likely the central heating than anything very critical.'

'So – what?'

But he had the whole top half of his body inside the cavity now, arms reaching deep. 'Oh, this is no good,' his muffled voice called.

'Problem?' Rose asked.

The Doctor emerged. 'Haven't got a lighter, have you? I need to keep the heat up on the pipe, make the water boil. The sonic screwdriver needs me there to hold the button down and I think Sally'll notice if I've got my head stuck in the wall.'

'No lighter,' Rose told him. 'Sorry.'

'Something combustible?' McCavity suggested. 'Paper, maybe?'

The Doctor shook his head, and Rose saw Dugg pushing his notebook quickly into his pocket. 'Need to maintain a constant, steady heat.'

Mirroring Dugg, Rose thrust her hands into her jacket pockets. 'How about...' she started, looking round for something that might work, but seeing nothing useful. 'How about...' Then she realised what was in her pocket. 'This!'

'Brilliant!' The Doctor snatched the matchstick from her and disappeared back inside the wall cavity. 'I can ignite it with the sonic,' he called. 'Well done, Rose.'

'That won't burn for long,' McCavity pointed out.

'You'd be surprised,' Rose told him. 'Everlasting match. Like Mickey wishes they had down the pub.'

McCavity had no chance to ask her what she meant. 'Time's up!' Sally shouted from the other side of the barricaded door.

'Tell her we'll open up,' the Doctor's muffled voice called back from inside the wall. 'Take down the barricade.'

'You sure?' McCavity said.

'Just do it.'

'Ignore him,' Rose said. 'When he's like this, you just

let him get on with it.' She raised her voice to shout, 'OK, we'll let you in. Just don't hurt Jimm.'

'How sweet,' Sally replied. 'But you'd better be quick.'

They pulled the chairs and table away. 'He's probably setting up a booby trap to spray them with hot steam or boiling water or something,' Rose reassured Dugg and McCavity.

'No, he isn't,' the Doctor said, helping them pull the table clear. The wall panel was pushed out of sight and a star chart covered the hole.

The door swung open to reveal the three robots – four including Sally. Jonesy, or rather Smithers as Rose now knew he was, held the unconscious Jimm in his arms.

'If you've harmed him…' the Doctor started, his voice dark, as Dugg took the boy and carried him into the room.

But Sally cut him off. 'You'll do nothing. And we haven't. He's merely unconscious. But now that you're all together, we can fix that.'

The other robots crowded closer, eagerly.

Then the noise started. At first it was a faint knocking sound from somewhere in the ship's infrastructure. But then it got louder, more insistent. Soon it was a heavy banging, like someone hammering a metal drum with a croquet mallet.

'What is that?' McCavity had his hands over his ears and was shouting to be heard.

The robots looked at each other, confused. It sounded to Rose like the knackered central heating when the boiler packed up in Mum's flat. She glanced at the Doctor, and he winked.

'Krarks!' he exclaimed loudly. 'Oh, my goodness, there must be a rupture on one of the external supply pipes. That's krarks we can hear, bashing into the pipes, trying to rip them apart.' Suddenly he was all sympathy. 'Oh, and you were doing so well,' he told Sally and the others. 'Just about to force us to look for Glint's ship and everything, and now some nasty krarks are about to tear your ship apart. We'll die when the hull is punctured and the air escapes. But I guess they'll rip you apart for the water and steam, which sounds rather unpleasant.' He sucked air through clenched teeth. 'Enjoy.'

The tall robot that was really Cannon-K was shuddering with the effort of trying to speak at last. 'Krarks!' it managed to say, voice rusty and flat.

'Yeah,' the Doctor agreed. 'Nasty. I suppose someone could... No, that would be just daft. Far too dangerous.'

'What?' Sally demanded.

'Yes, what?' Elvis/King echoed, barely heard above the hammering sound.

'Well...' The Doctor swallowed, as if what he was about to propose was insanely dangerous. 'Someone could go outside the ship and fix the ruptured pipe before they manage to tear it apart.'

'And how would you keep the krarks away while you do it?' Rose demanded, caught up in the Doctor's story. 'Er, sorry,' she added as he shot her an annoyed look.

But he was once again completely into the role as he turned back to Sally. 'With my sonic krark-repellent screwdriver. They can't stand the ultrasonics, it's well known. And it seems to be working again, just.'

Sally looked at the Doctor, then at the other robots. Then she looked back at the Doctor. 'And in return, you ask for – what?'

'Look, I can't say I fancy being killed by the krarks any more than you do. If it keeps us alive a bit longer, that's good enough for me. And if it earns Brownie points towards you reconsidering making us walk the space plank or whatever, then that's great too. But decide soon!' he shouted over the increasingly frantic hammering of the pipes.

'All right,' Sally shouted back. 'We'll get you suited up. And no tricks, or we kill the others, agreed?'

'Agreed,' the Doctor said. 'But stick them in the escape pod while I sort out the pipework.'

'Why?' Smithers rasped.

The Doctor looked at the robot as if it had belched at a dinner party. 'Why? Because if the ship depressurises before I get it repaired, then you lot will be fine and dandy, but my chums here will suffocate. So stick them in the pod, seal it up airtight, and they'll be safe and sound.'

'And have them escape?' Sally said. 'That's what escape pods do.'

'Not if you keep the clamps locked so it's attached to the main body of the ship,' the Doctor pointed out. 'And not, I hope, without me either. What's the problem? I'd have thought you'd like the idea. After all, the pod will make a great prison cell, don't you think?'

'Prison cell,' Sally agreed. 'Or coffin.'

The escape pod was surprisingly spacious, which McCavity explained was because they were frequently needed. That didn't exactly fill Rose with confidence. But she was still streets ahead of McCavity and Dugg, who both seemed convinced that the Doctor had gone to his death and that the rest of them would soon follow, one way or another.

Jimm was stirring. He fidgeted and called out in his drugged sleep, lying on a low curved bunk at the back of the pod. It was really just one circular room, and an airlock. McCavity's wooden space chest was pushed up against a wall where, Rose assumed, Dugg had dumped it after they boarded. Beside the chest, a small hatchway led into a tiny washroom, and there was a separate area at the 'front' of the pod that housed a miniature control panel – chunky levers and old-fashioned dials. McCavity explained that the pod could be piloted over short distances, and even had its own boiler.

'Not that they'll let us launch,' he said glumly. 'The safety catches are all still in place, locking us to the main ship.'

At which point there was a series of small explosions from the back of the pod and a drifting sensation. Rose felt suddenly light-headed. Light-footed too – as if she weighed only half of what she had a moment before.

'What was that?' she said.

'Er,' McCavity said. 'Sounded and felt like the safeties disengaging.' He ran to the single porthole above the control panel. 'They've cut us adrift, Larissa, my love. Marooned us.' His face was ashen.

Through the porthole, Rose could see the stars moving as the pod spun slowly round and the main ship came into sight.

'Don't see any krarks,' Dugg said, joining them by the controls.

'There aren't any. It was a trick,' Rose said.

'Oh?' He sounded both surprised and impressed.

'For all the good it did us,' McCavity complained. 'These controls are dead. They have to be activated from the main ship. And the Doctor has abandoned us. Assuming he's still alive.'

'He's still alive. He'll find us. He wouldn't leave us.'

'Then where is he?' McCavity roared. He grabbed Rose's shoulders and shook her. 'Where is he?'

She pulled back, surprised at his fury. 'He'll be here, all right? Trust me.'

'Trust?'

'What's going on?' Jimm said woozily from behind them. 'Where are we? Are we – hey! We're in space, aren't we?'

Rose looked round, smiled at Jimm to reassure him, and saw that he was already sinking back on to the bunk. 'Look,' she said quietly to McCavity, 'the Doctor hasn't just run off and left us. I know…' She hesitated, wondering how he'd take it. 'I know why you're worried about being abandoned, being left by your friends. But the Doctor's not like that. Not like…' She stopped. Maybe she was digging herself a hole.

'Not like my Larissa?' McCavity said, his voice dangerously quiet. 'Is that what you were going to say?' And now he was shouting. 'Is it?'

'No,' she shouted back. 'Yes,' she admitted more quietly. 'Look, sorry. I never knew her.'

'She was so lovely,' McCavity said, his voice quiet now but shaking with emotion. 'I loved her so much.' His eyes were moist as he stared at Rose. 'I really did, you know. Despite everything. But I couldn't… I just couldn't… I loved her so very much…' And suddenly he was crying, face in hands, sinking to his knees.

'Sorry,' Rose said quietly. 'I'm sorry, all right?' But she doubted if he heard her. 'Oh, hell, I'm sounding like Kevin the Apologetic Monster.'

Then the door opened. She heard it quite clearly. They were in the middle of space, floating through the vacuum, and someone had opened the door. Rose was not at all surprised to see that it was the Doctor, but that didn't stop her hugging him tight. Which was not as easy as it might have been as he was wearing what looked like a deep sea diver's suit, complete with a spherical brass helmet fitted with a small circular window at the front, criss-crossed with wire.

The door clanged shut and Dugg swung the locking wheel. The Doctor twisted the helmet and lifted it off.

'Phew, that's better.'

McCavity pulled himself to his feet, and Jimm was sitting up on the bunk again to see what was going on.

'No krarks, then?' Rose said.

'No krarks. It'll take them a while to work out what's happened.'

'When they do, they'll come after us and we're just drifting.'

'Not a problem.' He stripped off the loose-fitting spacesuit. 'I can sort out these controls and we can be on our way.' He strode over to the instrument panel and started fiddling.

'And what's to stop Salvo 7-50 and the others coming after us?' McCavity wanted to know. 'The main ship has far more power and speed than us.'

'Ah, but they don't know where we're going and we do. Yes, Rose,' he said without any hint of modesty, 'I know where Glint's ship is. Tracked it down, sorted it out, off to visit and get the T-shirt.'

He pulled a rolled-up chart from his inside coat pocket and unrolled it. Seeing nowhere to put it, he handed it to Dugg.

'They'll catch us,' McCavity said.

'Oh yes, eventually. They can follow the heat of our steam trail if they're quick about it. But they were kind enough to bung me out of an airlock right by their main engines. So they'll have to fix them first.' The pod shivered and turned slowly until they could no longer see the main ship. 'Off we go, then,' the Doctor announced.

'They're used to repairing damaged ships,' McCavity said. 'They'll come after us and kill us.'

'It'll be all right,' the Doctor insisted. 'Trust me. We know where Glint is, we're all safe and sound, and if it gets a bit hairy or if Sally and Co. look like catching up we can just escape in my now fully, or almost fully, functioning TAR–' He stopped in mid-flow and frowned. 'Where *is* the TARDIS?' he said to Rose. 'I made sure it was loaded into the escape pod for just this sort of eventuality, so we'd be quite safe. Safe as houses.'

'We're twice as safe,' Rose reminded him. 'Safe as two houses. And two escape pods, remember? The TARDIS is in the other one.'

SEVEN

It wasn't long before they started seeing the wrecks. The first was a huge cargo freighter – Galactic Seven class, according to Jimm, who stared in awe through the small porthole as they passed within a hundred yards of the hull. It was a long, fat, ugly slab of metal studded with antennae.

'How long's it been here?' Rose wondered.

'That type went out of service over a century ago,' Jimm told her.

As they reached the end of the ship, Rose could see two tiny shapes motionless next to the enormous engine pods – figures attached to the hull by thin cables.

'Trying to the last minute to repair the systems,' the Doctor said. 'Don't suppose they ever knew what hit them.'

'The zeg,' McCavity said. 'I've read accounts from people who were lucky enough to be rescued. The same pattern – first their communications are affected, then loss of power. The propulsion systems seem to suffer traumatic failure. And once the engines have stopped, they just drift. No navigation, no control, no idea where they are or where they're going. The lucky ones drift through and come out the other side before they run out of water or life support shuts down.'

'And the unlucky ones?' Rose asked quietly.

'Don't.'

The next ship was a small pleasure cruiser, hanging apparently motionless in the distance, its name stencilled on the side: *Blacklight*. Then another freighter, followed by a passenger liner. The whole of the side of the liner facing them as they passed was torn open, and Rose could see the streamlined shapes of krarks as they swam in and out of the holes.

'Hunting down the last pockets of air,' the Doctor said. 'Let's hope there's still some left in there for them.'

'Why?' Dugg said from the back of the group, watching over everyone else's heads, pen poised above notebook.

'Because otherwise we might become a tastier proposition, that's why.'

'Don't these ships see that they're heading into, like, a spaceship graveyard?' Rose asked.

'Most of them have been here for decades, centuries even,' McCavity said. 'The zeg's been properly mapped and charted now. But in the old days they just thought it was a minor systems failure at first. Till they lost control.'

'Space is very big,' the Doctor told her. 'There may be thousands of ships stranded at the edge of the zeg, and tens of thousands more deep within it. But that still means you can go for light years without seeing a single one.'

'You probably wouldn't see anything till you were well inside, and then it's too late,' Jimm agreed.

'Systems pack up,' the Doctor explained. 'But this is space – you keep going in a straight line. At least for a while. Gravity accumulation and minor collisions slow you down eventually. Venting oxygen and fluid, explosions as critical systems go under. Whatever – they all change the course and speed. So where the ships end up is haphazard and random. That's one reason why no one has ever found Glint's *Buccaneer*. Until now. Never mind a needle in a haystack, more like a grain of salt on a sandy beach.'

'So, if it's not a dumb question,' Rose said, 'are we nearly there yet?'

'I think we are,' the Doctor said. 'It's near the edge of the zone, so let's just hope that there's still some life support.'

'Is that important?' Jimm asked.

'Well, we only have one spacesuit,' the Doctor told him. 'And I've got first dibs on that.'

The *Buccaneer* was unmistakable and magnificent.

With its midnight-black hull, it was hard to see where the ship ended and space began. A silver skull was painted on the side: the eye sockets were gun ports and the mouth was the docking bay. Huge, pale solar sails stood proudly above the main structure, pitted and torn by meteorites or possibly krarks, although the hull itself seemed to be intact.

'Space galleon,' Rose commented, impressed.

'I thought the skull motif on the side was just a rumour, a story,' McCavity said. 'Part of the legend.'

'You'll need to update your model of it when you get back,' the Doctor joked. 'Colour scheme's been changed from the factory settings, and you haven't deployed the solar sails.'

'Yes,' McCavity agreed. He seemed completely serious. 'She's magnificent, isn't she, darling?'

Jimm just stared, awestruck. Dugg was again scribbling notes.

The Doctor manoeuvred the pod round to the other side of the *Buccaneer*. 'They'll know the ship when they see it, of course,' he said. 'But there's no point in advertising to Sally and her shipmates that we're here or where we docked.'

There was a standard emergency docking hatch close to the aft of the ship and the pod clanged into place. Steam hissed from the edge of the heavy, circular door. The pressure equalised and the Doctor punched the air in delight.

'Atmosphere,' he said. 'Probably a bit stale, but the

hull doesn't seem to be holed. Whether there's any light is another matter, though. Right, who's coming to find the treasure?'

The ship was lit with blood-red emergency lighting. Solar energy was converted direct to luminescence, so was unaffected by the zeg. But the doors all needed opening manually, pumping a lever set into the bulkhead to build pressure and operate the hydraulic mechanism. It reminded Rose of the crank-handle working of the TARDIS doors on Starfall.

The hatchway had opened into a narrow passage that connected to what seemed to be the main corridor running the length of the ship. McCavity led the way, down a stairwell to the lower level, where he claimed the secure hold – the vault – was located. That was where the treasure would be. The Doctor, Rose and Jimm followed and Dugg brought up the rear, carrying the wooden chest, which McCavity insisted would be useful to carry any treasure.

'At least life support's working,' the Doctor said. 'The ship's systems probably managed to shut down in a sensible manner without blowing a gasket or whatever. So the *Buccaneer*'s pretty much intact.'

'Lucky for us,' Rose commented.

They walked almost in silence, whispering or speaking in low voices as if Glint's ghost might be disturbed if they made too much noise. Jimm was constantly ooh-ing and ah-ing and pointing out the most ordinary features, while McCavity continued to mutter to his absent wife.

The corridor leading to what they hoped was the vault was carpeted and the walls were lined with wood panels. At intervals, empty frames hung on the walls.

'Hey,' Rose said, 'maybe we're not the first people here. Someone's nicked the pictures.'

'Holo-pics,' the Doctor told her. 'The frame projects a three-dimensional image. Except they're not working, of course. That's real, though,' he added rather needlessly, pointing to a pair of curved swords mounted on the wall. A shield with the grinning skull symbol hung beneath them.

'Let's hope the treasure's real too,' Rose said.

The Doctor didn't answer her. He just grinned rather disconcertingly.

The corridor ended in a large room. It was like the trophy room of a successful school or sports club. Except that the cases were full of weapons – from futuristic blasters to swords and daggers. More weapons hung on the walls, along with more of the empty holo-frames and several blackened and tarnished name plates from – presumably – ships that Glint had raided.

Several doors led off from the trophy room. But the one directly opposite them as they entered was a heavy metal door with a large locking wheel. It looked like the sort of door Rose would expect to find in the basement of the Bank of England.

'No prizes for guessing which door we want,' she said.

McCavity was already examining the door. 'There doesn't seem to be a lock,' he said. 'It's just for protection against damage to the ship.' He tried the wheel, but it refused to budge. 'Dugg, put that down and get this open, will you?'

The large man set down his load carefully next to one of the display cases and went to help with the door.

'What's he brought that for?' Rose said, staring in surprise at the space chest that Dugg had been carrying. 'Is he really hoping to take the treasure out in it or what?'

The Doctor shrugged. 'Who knows?'

'Is there really treasure in there?' Jimm asked excitedly. He was hopping from one foot to the other. 'Is there? Is there is there is there?'

'Yes,' the Doctor said, laughing. On the other side of the room, the heavy locking wheel was squealing in protest as Dugg persuaded it to turn. 'Yes yes yes. Well, maybe maybe maybe.'

Jimm laughed too, and soon Rose was laughing as well.

And the door was swinging massively open – slow and ponderous, as Dugg dragged it with all his weight. To reveal…

An empty room.

Or almost empty. It was a large, square, metal-lined box. The only thing in the room was a large casket – polished black, the size and shape of a coffin. A web of pipes and wires was inlaid in the lid like a complex pattern of engraving.

'Is that it?' Rose said. 'The Resurrection Casket?'

Dugg was walking slowly over to the sinister black object.

'Don't open it,' the Doctor said, joining him. His voice was quiet but full of authority. 'Whatever you do, don't open it. I don't know what happened to the take-the-money option, but don't open the box.'

'Why not?' Dugg said, standing in front of the casket now. 'Surely the treasure is inside.'

'No. Afraid not.'

Glancing round, as if to see if anyone was watching, the Doctor pulled his thick-rimmed spectacles from his top pocket. He carefully put them on, tapping the bridge with his index finger to push them right up. He ran his fingers over the top of the casket, feeling the texture and examining how the pipework was laid into the lid.

'And if the stories are true,' he went on, 'you'd be releasing the most dangerous, murderous, bloodthirsty and unpleasant pirate who ever flew the spaceways. That's a good reason not to open it.'

Dugg thought about this. 'Fair point,' he decided.

Jimm and McCavity were both in the room, staring at the complete lack of treasure. For the first time, Jimm looked disappointed. The Doctor and Rose joined him, and the Doctor slapped him on the back. 'Never mind, eh?' he said. 'Who wants to be rich anyway?'

McCavity was both confused and furious. 'Where is it?' he demanded. 'Where's the treasure? Over twenty years of piracy and nothing to show for it? That cannot be! Is this what we've dreamed of all these years, Larissa? An empty room? Who has taken it? Who's been here and taken the treasure?' he roared.

'Er, well, actually,' said a deep, gruff voice from the doorway behind them. 'I could probably have saved you a trip. If you'd only asked.'

McCavity just stared.

Rose and Jimm turned slowly to see who was speaking.

'Hello, Kevin,' said the Doctor, whipping off his glasses and putting them away.

The huge shaggy form of Kevin was leaning against the doorframe. As Rose watched, it wiped a massive paw across its face and she saw that its mouth was dripping with something red and viscous.

'Oh, gross!' she said out loud before she could stop herself.

'What?' the monstrous creature said. Then it saw what had rubbed off on the back of its paw. 'Oh, that. Sorry.' It licked the red goo from its fur and smacked its lips in appreciation. 'Ketchup,' Kevin explained. 'From my kronkburger. I was just watching a holo-vid. Can't watch vids without a snack. Kronkburger and a big can of cooler. That does it for me.' The big furry figure pushed away from the door and wandered into the room. 'Bit of a blow, this, I s'pose. All this way and no treasure.' Kevin shook his head sadly.

'What are *you* doing here?' McCavity hissed angrily.

'Well, pardon me, but I live here. Where did you think I went in between my little assignments? This is my home. I didn't think you were offering free accommodation with the job, and I don't just curl up inside some old lamp or urn, you know.'

'Job?' Rose echoed. 'Now, hang on – does that mean…'

The Doctor took her arm. 'I think our friend Kevin is in the employ of Mr McCavity here. Am I right?' he asked McCavity. 'Or am I right? Tell me I'm right.'

'Quite right.' Some of the man's self-assurance was returning and he was looking, Rose thought, dangerously smug. 'The Shadow Creature is in my thrall.'

'Ooh,' the Doctor said, sounding impressed. 'In your thrall, is he? How grand. I bet you're really chuffed, Kevin.'

'Oh yeah,' Kevin said, with no attempt to disguise his sarcasm. 'Chance of a lifetime. Prospects for promotion, pension plan, even healthcare. I don't think.'

'Kevin?' McCavity said, confused.

'What about it?' Kevin demanded. 'It's my name *actually*. Not that you ever even bothered to ask. I quite like my name, and I don't take kindly to people calling me something else. It's demeaning, you know. But oh no, it's Creature of Shadows do my bidding this,

Spawn of Darkness harken to my will on that. I mean, have you heard yourself? Have you?'

'McCavity sent Kevin to kill those people?' Rose said.

'And me,' the Doctor said, miffed. 'Don't forget me. I seriously upset him. More seriously than I'd realised. But then he decided I was more use alive to lead him to the –' he paused to look round the empty room – 'treasure.'

McCavity was red-faced with anger now. Jimm, by contrast, was talking eagerly to Kevin.

'You were Hamlek Glint's creature, weren't you? When he put the Black Shadow on people, you went and got them. Oh, that's just so cool!'

Kevin looked down at the small boy modestly. He inspected his claws. 'Well, it was just a job, you know. But I do pride myself on doing it well.'

'Yet you allowed him to escape,' McCavity finally managed to splutter, pointing at the Doctor.

'Yeah, well, the job wasn't properly specced, was it? Not my fault, O Master of All Things.'

'But why?' Rose demanded. 'Why did you kill them?'

'Orders,' Kevin said with a sniff. 'Nothing I can do. More than my hide's worth. Seemed a bit of a shame, though. I mean, cut-throat bloodthirsty pirates and space villains – even Space Revenue Officers, that's one thing. But a few old codgers passing off dodgy silverware does seem a bit drastic.'

'Wasn't all dodgy, though, was it?' the Doctor said. His eyes were fixed firmly on McCavity. 'If they'd just tried to rip you off, they might have been all right. But they brought you something genuine. Years ago. And so you were deeply, deeply disappointed when this time it was all a sham.' He walked slowly towards McCavity, who backed away. 'So what was it? What was the key that allowed you to control Kevin? Ancient scroll? Dusty book? Special hat perhaps? Do you have to wear a special hat? I do so hope so. Oh, don't tell me it's a wand.'

McCavity had his back to the wall now. He was clutching at his throat, and Rose thought he was having some sort of attack. But he was struggling to pull a chain round his neck. On it was a large, plain, gold medallion. 'This,' he spluttered. 'This is the key. So be very careful, Doctor. I have the power of life and death over you – over you all.'

The Doctor stopped in mid-step. 'Ah,' he said. 'You've got it with you. That's… good.'

'He still has to put the Black Shadow on you,' Jimm said, running to stand with the Doctor. 'Just don't take anything from him, or let him put it in your pocket.'

'Or offer him pencil and paper,' Rose suggested. 'Dugg, take note. No, not literally, I mean.' She sighed and shook her head. 'Never mind.'

But McCavity's face had twisted into a nasty sneer. 'I've had them pre-printed anyway,' he said.

'Yeah, but what'd be the point of killing us now?' the Doctor said. 'No treasure. And we're not the threat, we're on your side, remember. It's Sally Salvo and her chums you need to watch out for.'

'Salvo 7-50?' Kevin said. The Doctor nodded. Kevin did not seem pleased. 'Oh, do me a favour. What's she after? I thought she was long gone, melted down for scrap. Nothing but trouble, she is – take it from me.'

'We got that, thanks,' Rose told him.

'So where is she, then?' Kevin asked.

'Miles away,' the Doctor said. 'Stranded in space with no engines. They'll get them repaired eventually, but I don't expect them to show up here for a good while yet.'

As he finished speaking, the whole room shook and the ship echoed with a loud metallic clang.

'What was that?' Rose said, struggling to regain her balance.

'Sounded and felt like a ship docking,' Dugg said. 'Who do you reckon…' He broke off and frowned. 'Oh.'

'They got going again in time to follow our trail of steam. Expect the unexpected,' the Doctor said. 'I should know that by now. Maybe I do and it slipped my mind. Rats!'

EIGHT

On Kevin's advice, they decided to move. None of them fancied being stuck in the vault, and the trophy room had too many doors.

'Back to the escape pod?' Jimm suggested.

'And meet our robotic friends coming the other way? They'll know where we are and where we'll try to get to,' the Doctor said. 'They know this ship backwards. And, worst luck, forwards too.'

'What, then?' Rose demanded. 'Wait here for Robo-Psycho and her mates?'

'We need a room that's easy to defend, with a back door for escape when and if necessary,' the Doctor said. 'Any idea?'

'Games room,' Kevin suggested. 'Fits the bill, and if we get bored I'll give you a game of billiards.'

The Doctor grinned. 'You know, that sounds ideal.'

'Come on, then,' Rose said. 'They'll be here soon.'

'And they won't be happy the treasure has gone,' Jimm said. 'Unless they took it?'

The Doctor shook his head. 'They didn't. Because they needed brilliant me to bring them here. Which was a bit daft, but we'll let that pass for now. And they're also after Glint.'

'What for?' McCavity asked.

'Well,' the Doctor replied, 'let me see now. He did sort of betray them, abandon them and give instructions they were to be melted down for scrap. So I imagine they want to revive him from his casket and then sit down with a few drinks and nibbles for a chat about the good old days. What do you reckon?'

McCavity considered this. 'Point taken,' he said. 'Dugg, you'd better bring the Resurrection Casket.'

'Why?' Dugg asked. 'Won't they just take it and go?'

'They might,' the Doctor said. 'But apart from the fact they'll revive the homicidal Mr Glint, they might also want to ask us where their treasure's gone. He's right for once in his life – bring the casket. If nothing else, it'll give us something to bargain with.'

'Right.' Dugg lifted one end of the black casket, struggling with the weight. 'Er, I'll need a hand,' he said.

'Oh, for goodness' sake,' Kevin grumbled. He lumbered across the room and pushed Dugg aside, taking the casket. He lifted it easily on to his shoulder and led the way from the vault. 'If you want a job doing...' Rose heard him muttering as he went past.

'You bring that,' McCavity said to Dugg, pointing to his space chest.

'And what will you be bringing?' Rose asked him over-politely.

McCavity met her stare, and smiled. He was holding something up – a small piece of parchment. In the middle of it was shaded a dark shape. 'Unless you'd like to carry it for me?' he asked quietly.

Rose swallowed, aware that Kevin had paused in the doorway and was watching them. He looked sadly at Rose, and for a moment she could imagine him apologising to her. Before he ripped her arms off.

'That's OK,' Rose said. 'I'm sure you'll manage.' She breathed a sigh of relief as McCavity nodded and followed the others to the door.

Kevin led them all down a short corridor, then through a large living area to another room beyond. There was a big screen on one wall, with a sofa against the opposite wall. A bag of what looked like popcorn had spilled over beside the sofa. A square dartboard was on another wall; low tables with dusty magazines and things that looked like mobile phones were dotted about. The middle of the room was taken up with what looked like a snooker table, only with extra pockets along the sides. It seemed to have been left in the middle of a game.

'Sorry about the mess,' Kevin said, brushing the balls aside and setting down the casket on the snooker table. 'Wasn't expecting visitors. Not after all this time.'

Dugg plonked McCavity's space chest down beside

the coffin-shaped black box. 'We could just maybe peek inside,' he said, tapping the Resurrection Casket.

'No,' the Doctor told him emphatically. 'We maybe just couldn't. No peeking inside the Resurrection Casket, all right? Now, where's that lead?' he asked, pointing to the door at the back of the room.

'Aft section,' Kevin said. 'Couple of state rooms, engines, main computer suite.'

'No other way to get there and take us by surprise?'

'Don't think so. Anyway, make yourselves at home, barricade the door or whatever, and I'll catch up with you later,' Kevin told them. 'If you're lucky.'

'Where are you going?' Jimm asked.

'Don't really fancy meeting Salvo and the gang again for a reunion,' Kevin confessed. 'So I'll just slip out of this dimension until it's all over, if that's OK with you.'

'It isn't,' McCavity snapped. 'We need you here.' He was holding out the medallion, the chain tight round his neck as he thrust the circle of gold towards Kevin. 'By the power I hold, by the Dominion of Darkness and Shadows, I order you to stay here.'

Rose could hear the capital letters.

'By the power I hold,' Kevin mimicked. 'Dominion of Darkness blah blah blah. Why not just ask? I can see the power. I know about the power. And yes, all right, I'll stay. Or, if you prefer, I am duty bound by that power vested in you by virtue of the Shadow Medallion to obey, O Master, until such time as my duty be discharged or you release me from my bonds or you are divested of the power that binds me to thy will. Blah blah blooming blah.'

'Yes,' the Doctor said. 'Well, I'm glad that's clear. Let's get the door blocked up as best we can.'

'Then what?' Rose asked.

'Maybe we can bargain with them.'

'For what?'

The Doctor shrugged. 'Oh, I dunno. Maybe they'll lock us up in the other escape pod.'

Rose nodded. 'And maybe,' she said, 'they won't.'

On McCavity's instruction, Kevin helped shift the snooker table over to block the door. To be on the safe side, they then stacked tables and chairs on top of it, pulling the two caskets to the other end of the large table.

'Perhaps they won't find us,' Jimm said. 'If we're quiet, maybe they won't know we're here.'

At that point, the snooker table shuddered as someone – something – tried to open the door. A chair slipped from the precarious pile and fell to the floor.

'They know we're here,' Rose said.

Moments later, Sally's voice came from the other side of the door. 'This is becoming a bit of a habit, isn't it? Now, let us in to claim what's ours and then we'll leave you in pieces.'

'Doesn't she mean "leave us in peace"?' Dugg said.

'I don't think so,' the Doctor replied.

'We don't have long,' McCavity said. He gripped the Doctor's arm, turning him round so they were facing each other. 'We have to open the Resurrection Casket.'

'No,' the Doctor said simply.

'We *have* to.'

'Why?'

McCavity blinked. 'So we have something to bargain with.'

'We've got the casket,' Rose said. 'Why do we need Glint himself? He's safely out of it right now.'

'And what if we need the casket?' McCavity shouted at her. 'What if they get in here and kill us? What then? We need the casket open and working so we can bargain, so they know they can't kill us.'

'That's long enough,' Sally's voice shouted from behind the door. 'Either you come out now or we're coming in. You can't run and hide for ever.'

'Nothing wrong with getting a good head start, though,' Rose said.

'They *can* kill us,' the Doctor said quietly. 'And they know it.'

'But with the casket…' McCavity insisted.

'Yes,' Jimm said. 'We could just get inside – get put inside – and we'd come out well again. Completely recovered.'

'No,' the Doctor said forcefully. 'Why is this difficult to understand? Am I speaking Martian Sanskrit or something? No, got it? No!'

'You mean "No, don't do it" or "No, we won't come

out again all better"?' Rose asked.

The Doctor blinked, then ran a hand through his less than tidy hair. 'Both. I think. Even without letting Glint out of his box, it doesn't work like that.' He was having to shout now above the pounding on the door. The snooker table was shaking under each impact, but staying in place.

'It can bring us back to life – that's what resurrection means!' McCavity shouted back.

'Maybe it is, but that's not what this casket does.' The Doctor was at the table, tracing the path of one of the patterns on the lid of the black coffin-shaped casket. 'Revive maybe, but not resurrect. Keep in cryo-stasis perhaps, but no one comes back from the dead.' He caught Rose's eye. 'Almost no one.'

'Are you saying it doesn't work?' McCavity was staring at the Doctor open-mouthed.

'Heal your wounds maybe. DNA extrapolation for repair and rejuvenation even, perhaps. But an honest to goodness back from the dead Lazarus job? I doubt it. Maybe if the DNA's still active and you're not actually brain dead. But when Sally gets through that door with her mates we're not just going to need stuffing into a casket, we're going to need gluing back together first and I really don't think this box of tricks is up to the job. All right?'

'It has to be,' McCavity said. 'It must. It has to bring people back from the dead.' He grabbed the Doctor's lapels and pulled him close, shouting at him from point-blank range. 'Don't you understand? You have to make it work.'

'Don't *you* understand? I can't!' the Doctor shouted back.

'Make it work or you're dead.' He was waving the Black Shadow parchment in the Doctor's face.

'Why is it so important?' the Doctor demanded. 'Why are you suddenly so intent on coming back to life when, in case you'd not noticed, we're not even dead yet?'

'Just open the casket!' McCavity yelled.

'Why?' the Doctor yelled back.

The door shifted, opening just an inch. But it was enough. The snooker table juddered. Chairs and a heavy wooden table piled on top slipped and fell, knocking into the black casket. The Resurrection Casket slid along the table, catching the corner of McCavity's space chest and knocking it backwards.

The space chest caught against the raised, padded cushion at the edge of the table, tipping up. For a second it looked as if it was going to settle back down against the cushion. But then the attack on the door was renewed and more chairs slipped from the pile. They avalanched down, knocking into the top of the angled chest and tipping it further.

'No – Larissa!' McCavity shouted as he saw the chest begin to topple sideways. He let go of the Doctor and ran.

But too late. The tables shifted again and the chest

fell from the snooker table. It crashed to the floor and the bracket holding the padlock burst, falling away. The lid opened, spilling the contents of the chest across the floor.

Rose's hand flew to her mouth. Dugg took a step backwards. Jimm shrieked in surprise and fear. Kevin rolled his eyes and the Doctor nodded sadly at the bizarre, horrific sight. 'Shouldn't have opened the box,' the Doctor said quietly.

McCavity was on his knees beside the chest. The blackened, fragile skeleton that had tumbled out lay shattered across the floor, spilling out of the tattered, rotting remains of a blood-red velvet dress. Sightless skull-eyes stared back at McCavity, like the emblem on the side of the ship.

'Larissa,' McCavity gasped. 'Oh, Larissa, I'm so sorry.'

And between the skull's eyes, up on the forehead, Rose could clearly see the hole where she instinctively knew the bullet had drilled into the woman's brain.

'I'll bring you back,' McCavity was sobbing. 'I'll bring you back to life, my darling. I love you so much. It will all be all right this time, I promise. Everything will be all right again. Like it used to be.' He was cradling what was left of her in his arms, rocking back and forth on his knees as he cried. 'Like it used to be, before...'

'Before you killed her?' the Doctor said coldly. 'She never ran off with the Captain of the Watch at all, did she? Jealousy, was it? Found them together, did you?

Somehow you learned what they were planning and you got to her first. So what did you do to…' His voice trailed away and the colour seemed to drain from his face.

McCavity stared back at the Doctor, cheeks tear-stained but eyes burning with hatred. 'Yes, I found out,' he snarled. 'But she loved me. I know she did. Before he poisoned her mind. And as soon as you make the casket work we'll be together again.'

But the Doctor was looking at him in horror. 'The Captain of the Watch,' he said. 'The death of Captain Lockhardt, in your gallery. I knew there was something grotesque about that thing. It isn't a sculpture at all, is it? His name may not have been Lockhardt, but it's the captain all right. The fear and terror in his face, that's all too real.'

'You should have heard him scream,' McCavity said. He seemed to be talking to the skeleton. 'As the molten lead burned the life out of him. Oh, it was so beautiful. I only wish you could have been there, my darling. To see what I did for you.'

'Did for *her*?' Rose said, aghast. 'You killed her – shot her through the head.'

'It was for the best,' McCavity insisted. 'I had to do it. For *us*.'

Kevin cleared his throat. He was shaking his shaggy head and tutting. 'No prizes for spotting the real monster round here, then,' he said.

Rose put her arm round Jimm's shoulder. The boy

was staring in horrified disbelief at McCavity and the skeletal remains of his wife, Larissa. 'Are you OK?' Rose asked the boy.

He nodded but did not answer.

'What do you think, then?' the Doctor asked him. 'About all this? About McCavity and what he's been up to. About drenching the man who stole his wife – perhaps his whole life from him – drenching him in burning metal?'

'Doctor!' Rose hissed at him. 'Leave the boy alone.'

'Just interested in his point of view,' the Doctor complained. 'A fresh perspective. It's as valid as anyone's.' He turned back to Jimm, his eyes dark and deep. 'So, what d'you reckon, then?'

Jimm was still transfixed, still staring at McCavity. 'I think…' He swallowed and turned away. 'I think it's horrible.'

He pushed his head into Rose's shoulder and she held him close, felt him trembling. She glared at the Doctor. 'What're you doing?' she mouthed at him angrily.

But he ignored her. Instead he patted Jimm gently on the shoulder. 'I think it's horrible too,' he said quietly. 'Well done.'

McCavity had set down his wife's remains and was picking up the wooden chest. He opened the lid before placing the skeleton back inside – carefully, reverently. He closed the lid and then spent a moment just looking at it. He drew a deep breath and turned to the Doctor.

Behind him the snooker table juddered again and moved away from the door. A metallic arm was pushing its way through the narrow gap, feeling round to try to move the obstruction, shoving chairs out of the way but unable to move the table.

'You'd better start hiding in there,' Sally's voice called out mockingly. 'Run and hide, because I'm counting to a hundred. Maybe I'll only get to fifty before we start looking. We're coming to get you, ready or not.'

'Yes, Doctor,' McCavity said, his voice threateningly quiet. 'Run and hide. Because if you won't make the Resurrection Casket work, if you won't bring her back, then you'll be the one needing it.' He walked slowly towards the Doctor, oblivious to the noise from the door, to the way the heavy snooker table was moving slowly but inexorably backwards, scraping across the floor.

'I've told you – that isn't how it works,' the Doctor said.

McCavity held a slip of parchment. He turned it over and over in his hand, Kevin watching closely. 'So, you won't help,' he said with contempt. 'Very well…' Then he paused. 'No, I have a better idea.'

'I hope it's to do with how we stop Sally and the robots from getting in here and killing us all,' the Doctor told him.

Across the room, Jimm and Rose and Dugg were now pushing at the table, trying to shove it back and close the door. But it wasn't moving. At best they were preventing it from opening further.

But McCavity seemed not to care. 'Let's see if you are willing to make the casket work for someone else, shall we? If not for me, if not for Larissa, then what about Jimm? Or Rose?'

He turned, the parchment held ready to push into the pocket of one of them. Rose stepped in front of Jimm, glaring at McCavity – daring him to give her the paper.

But the Doctor grabbed the man's arm and pulled him back. 'Listen,' he shouted in McCavity's ear. 'Just pay attention to someone else for a change, will you? I can't use the casket to bring back Larissa. Not *won't*, but *can't*. That's not how it works. It's probably based on a cloning technique using DNA sampling and reconstituting the subject from living tissue. Got that? *Living* tissue. And there's nothing left even remotely alive in that box of yours. Got it now? She's gone. For ever. She's dead. And *you* killed her.'

McCavity pulled away, shaking off the Doctor's grip. 'Then you deserve to die, Doctor,' he said. 'You know I'm a killer, so that shouldn't surprise you.' He turned, picked up his space chest and walked away, across the room, towards the door to the engineering section.

And the Doctor realised that McCavity was no longer holding the parchment.

The snooker table seemed to buckle, the end by the door rising up like a wave before crashing down again.

The whole table shot back a yard, sending Jimm and Rose tumbling to the floor. Dugg struggled to hold it, but was forced several paces back.

'Goodbye, Doctor,' McCavity shouted above the noise.

The noise of Salvo 7-50, Elvis, Smithers and Cannon-K shoving their way into the room, shouting in scraping metallic triumph.

The Doctor turned from the door and found Kevin looking down at him sadly. 'What?' the Doctor said.

'He put the Black Shadow in your coat pocket, Doctor,' Kevin said. 'Once you've been got with the Black Shadow, that's it, I'm afraid. Neat technicality last time, but it won't work again for you. The only other thing you can do is to return it to the person who put it on you, or get him to willingly release you from it. But it looks like McCavity's long gone. Sorry.'

'You don't have to do this,' the Doctor said.

Massive hairy paws loomed above him, claws glinting in the blood-red lighting.

'I do, I'm afraid,' Kevin said. 'Sorry, Doctor. I'm *really* sorry about this. But, hey – let's make it quick, eh?' And the claws slashed down.

NINE

Rose turned in time to see the Doctor throw himself to one side. He landed on the sofa, rolled and was at once back on his feet.

'Get the Resurrection Casket!' he yelled at Rose. 'Don't let them have it. And Jimm – action figures!' Then in a blur of speed he was out of the back door, Kevin close behind.

'Kevin!' Rose shouted.

The monster paused halfway to the door and turned back. 'Kind of busy,' he growled.

'Help us keep them out!'

Kevin sighed and shook his head. 'Wasn't told to fight them, just help barricade the door. Sorry.' Then his deep-set red eyes widened as he saw Sally struggling to push past the snooker table that was still blocking the robots' way.

'Oh, corks!' the monster exclaimed, and dived behind the sofa.

Rose could see the faint glow of his red eyes as he

watched nervously from his hiding place. 'Monsters hiding behind the sofa.' She shook her head. 'You see it all in this life.' Then she shouted at Dugg, 'Get the casket out of here. We'll hold them back as long as we can.'

Sally and the other robots still had to move the table to get properly into the room. Once Dugg let go, grabbing the black coffin-shaped casket and pulling it free, the table started to move again. The casket was so heavy that he had to drag it, grunting and straining and shouting with anger and adrenaline as he manhandled it out of the door.

'Now what?' Jimm asked, face pale and eyes wide. 'We can't fight them.'

He had a point, Rose had to admit. And now Elvis was pushing his way through under the table, while Cannon-K was climbing over it. 'We have to,' she said.

'Then we need a weapon. We can't just use our bare hands. They're battle robots. They're invincible.'

'Balls!' Rose told him. Jimm looked surprised. 'Snooker balls. Quick – help me with this, will you?' She was tearing urgently at the green baize covering the table, pulling at it where it folded into a pocket.

'Why do we need that?'

'We don't,' she told him. 'We need the cushion – the rubber underneath.' The pool table at the pub where Mickey watched the football was old and tattered and one of the cushions was so worn that you could see the black rubber beneath – a long strip of it. Same here, she was relieved to see, as she clawed her way through the baize and dragged out the length of cushion.

'Catapult!' Jimm realised.

'Get the balls,' she told him.

Kevin seemed to have gone from behind the sofa, so they dragged it quickly to block the back door, ducking down on the other side of it, in the doorway. Jimm tipped the snooker balls out of his shirt, which he'd pulled out to use as a makeshift basket. Rose threaded the strip of rubber through a hinge of the door on one side and the clasp that held it shut on the other. Then she knotted it into a loop.

'What did he mean about action figures?' she asked as she dragged the rubber back down the passage, expecting it to snap at any moment. If the knot didn't slip.

'I have figures of them all,' Jimm said. 'But I don't know how that helps.'

Elvis was tangled in a mass of tables and chairs that had fallen when the snooker table shifted. Cannon-K was coming at them now, forcing his way over the table and sending more furniture crashing down round the protesting Elvis. Sally and Smithers shouted encouragement as they continued to try to shift the table out of the way.

'So you know these robots, how they work, how they fit together. How the toys fit together anyway,' Rose said. But Jimm was right, she didn't see how that helped.

'Cannon-K,' Jim said, suddenly grinning. 'His head comes off. Uncle Bobb says it's just like the real thing, so maybe that's it. The neck, look, it's really thin.'

'Weak point.' Rose was struggling to hold the rubber tight. 'Let's see if we can aim this thing. Give me a ball, quick. Then get down.' She couldn't hold on for much longer.

Jimm reached for the pile of balls on the sofa. Cannon-K was almost on them. Jimm's hand froze in indecision.

'What colour do you want?'

The Doctor was running. He didn't have a plan as such, more of a list of To Do's. He had to find McCavity and persuade the man to take the Black Shadow off him – or he could pass it to McCavity and get Kevin off his case. Then he would be free to return and help Rose and Jimm and Dugg without fear of getting his head ripped off.

And assuming he could get them all away from Sally and the robots, they then needed to return to the ship and find the TARDIS. Probably that would mean they had to destroy the robots, which posed a bit of a challenge. But then, what was life without a few challenges?

He was tempted to revise his opinion when a sharp, heavy sword cut through the air from behind him and bit into the wall of the corridor close to his head. The Doctor had not noticed the doorway, let alone

McCavity lying in wait. He leaped back as McCavity struggled to pull the sword free for another swipe.

'Can't you give it a rest?' the Doctor demanded.

'If that creature can't kill you, I will,' McCavity snapped back, finally wrenching the blade free.

The Doctor backed slowly away, looking deep into McCavity's eyes and not liking what he saw there. 'You really are completely unhinged, aren't you?' he said. 'None of this north-north-west rubbish, I was wrong there. For once. You're the whole compass, you are.'

The sword sliced again, and again the Doctor managed to avoid it. Just. He was backing away along the corridor, keeping a close watch on McCavity as the man came at him once more.

'You want to talk about this?' the Doctor asked. The blade slashed again, catching the Doctor's coat and leaving a razor-cut across the chest. 'Thought not. Pity.' Abandoning all pretence of cool, the Doctor ran.

But not away from McCavity – straight at him. His shoulder caught the man as the sword was at the top of its arc, driving McCavity back down the corridor. When the Doctor stopped abruptly, McCavity kept going as if hit by a truck. He flew backwards, crashing to the ground. The sword was knocked from his grasp and clattered down beside him.

The Doctor spared it a glance – too far from him. He'd never get to it before McCavity, so there was no point in trying. The Doctor was running again, this time away from McCavity, down the corridor towards the engineering section. 'I don't really do "dull and boring and uneventful",' the Doctor muttered to himself. 'But there are days…'

Once the thing was moving, it was fairly easy to keep moving. It was when Dugg stopped that things got difficult. There was no question of taking the casket very far. Best to hide it somewhere. There were doors off the corridor, but most of them led into small storerooms, and it would only need one of the robots to open the door and they'd see the thing.

But Dugg knew he couldn't get far before they came after him, and he could hear the shouts from back down the corridor and knew the boy and Rose would need his help if they were to have any chance. He was a bodyguard, that was his job, and while Dugg had no wish to die he did want to do his job properly. And he was more inclined to guard the girl and the lad than McCavity, now he'd seen what the man had made him carry through the ship…

Maybe the next door. Soon, though, soon he would have to leave the casket and go back and help. Just keep moving… With that thought, he bumped into something large and heavy and unyielding, and stopped dead.

Swearing, Dugg turned to see what he'd walked backwards into. It was the enormous, dark furry form of Kevin.

'Honestly,' Kevin said, 'you big wuss. Give me that

and you get off out of it.'

Dugg gulped and nodded. He watched Kevin lift the heavy casket as if it weighed next to nothing.

'What are you waiting for?' Kevin asked.

'They need help. I'm going back,' Dugg told him.

Kevin watched the big man hurry back towards the games room. 'That's very noble,' Kevin said. 'Completely bonkers, but very noble.'

The first ball had whizzed past Cannon-K's shoulder and embedded itself in the wall behind.

'Close,' Jimm said, jumping up and down in excitement as he picked another ball.

'Not close enough.' Rose's arms ached from dragging the rubber strip back.

'Try blue this time.'

She held the blue snooker ball in the rubber and staggered backwards again, struggling to hold on and to aim at the robot, which was now perilously close to the sofa. Jimm ducked down low, and she prayed she wouldn't slip and hit him instead. She closed her eyes and let go.

The sound of the impact was tremendous – a metallic ringing like a broken bell being hit with a steel pole. Rose opened her eyes and saw that Cannon-K's head was dented on one side. He was clutching at it in what might have been disbelief. But while he had halted his advance, Sally, Elvis and Smithers were all now close behind.

'Good shot!' Jimm was shouting. 'Try the black, try the black. Aim for the neck. With the black.'

'Aim!' She could barely pull the rubber this time and it stretched nothing like as far as it had the first time before Rose was forced to let it go.

But that might have helped her aim. The black ball caught Cannon-K full in his thin neck. The heavy helmet-like head snapped back, as if in surprise. There was a wrenching, tearing sound, and it pulled free and fell to the floor.

'Well, that's just great,' a rasping robotic voice said. It took Rose a moment to realise it was Cannon-K's head, staring at her like the skull that had fallen from McCavity's space chest.

Sally was watching Rose and Jimm with an expression of pure contempt. 'That's enough mucking about,' she said. 'Elvis, Smithers, time to online.'

'What about me?' Cannon-K's head demanded.

'We'll fix you up later,' Smithers said. 'Just like the old days, eh? Sooner we get Glint back the better.'

'You won't get the casket,' Rose shouted at them. 'We know you just want revenge on Glint. We can do a deal.'

'Revenge?' Sally said. One side of her face seemed to find the idea funny.

'For selling you off for scrap,' Jimm told her.

'Oh, that.' Rose could almost hear the indifferent shrug in Sally's voice. 'Happens.'

'What?' Rose said in disbelief. 'You don't care?'

'Glint always knew best. If our days were numbered, then that's his choice. He was captain. It was his decision. That's why we want the casket, that's why we want Glint. Because he was the best. He *is* the best.'

As Sally spoke, she was walking slowly towards the sofa and ignoring Rose as she dragged back the strip once more, this time with a red ball in position. But it wasn't Sally that Rose and Jimm were watching.

Behind their commander, Elvis and Smithers were pulling plates of metal from their chests, removing cladding and panels from their limbs. Disconnecting the tiny steam engines and valves and pipes that drove them.

'There's still power here,' Elvis said. 'Not enough to move the ship, but enough for basic operations.'

'Yeah,' Smithers agreed. 'Basic stuff. Like sensory perception and movement.' He pulled off a breastplate to reveal the stained metal below – lights and mechanisms gleamed and glinted. There was the sound of systems powering up like a computer coming on. 'Like walking. And killing.'

Elvis pulled his thin metal face plate away, and beneath was the face that Rose remembered from Bobb's photo of the crew.

'The gloves are off,' Sally said. She lifted her artificial arm and removed the metal gauntlet. Beneath, her fingers were sharp blades, whirring and glowing. 'Sadly the damage is so great that most of my systems will have to stay steam-driven. For now. Till Smithers can fix me up and I can lose this substandard organic componentry.'

'That's someone's body you're talking about,' Rose said. 'Someone's face.'

Sally laughed. 'Not any more. It's mine now. Finders, keepers. But first things first.'

'Glint,' Elvis said. 'And when we get him out of his box he can lead us again. Like in the good old days. Death and blood and glory!'

'There's nothing like it!' Smithers agreed. 'Let's start now!' He set off towards the sofa, and this time there was no antiquated clanking or hissing of steam. This time a fully functioning pirate death robot strode purposefully towards them, servos whirring and hydraulics humming.

'You run, I'll hold them off.'

Rose thought it was Jimm who had spoken. But when a large beefy hand took the rubber strip from her and pulled it further back down the corridor she realised it was Dugg.

'Go on,' he said. 'Get out of here quick. Find the Doctor. He'll know what you should do.'

Rose grabbed Jimm and pulled him back and down to the floor as Smithers leaped easily over the sofa and Dugg released the snooker ball. The ball caught Smithers high in the chest and he was thrown back over the sofa, crashing to the ground in a shower of sparks.

'What about you?' Rose shouted to Dugg as she and Jimm ran.

Dugg was already stretching the makeshift catapult again. 'I know what I should do,' he replied. 'I'll give you as long as I can.' He paused, holding the catapult in one hand and reaching into his pocket with the other. He pulled out his notebook and threw it to Rose. 'My life's work,' he said. 'Look after it for me.'

She caught the book and held it tight. 'I'll give it back to you later,' she said.

Dugg laughed and took aim. 'Course you will,' he said.

The main engine room was a mass of pipes and cables. Air-tight lockers and equipment safes stood like sentinels between the sleeping reactors. As most of the rest of the ship, it was lit red like some ancient creature's forbidden lair.

The Doctor was making his way slowly between two of the cooling units. The systems were ticking over and so the coolant was still cold enough for a faint mist to be drifting from the tanks, tinged orange in the red light. He was heading as quietly as he could for the side wall – where a fire axe hung in a glass case. Whether it would be any use against McCavity's sword, he didn't know. But he had little choice and it had to be better than the alternative. Because the alternative was nothing.

He was almost there, reaching out to see how the case opened, when the sword smashed down from above. McCavity was on top of a cooling tank, legs astride as he hacked viciously down at the Doctor.

The Doctor leaped away, just in time, and the sword slammed into the tank. It clanged off at an angle, nicking a tiny hole through which a jet of mist spat out. Unbalanced by the glancing blow, McCavity stumbled. The Doctor grabbed the sword, almost crying out as he felt it cut into his hand, and pulled.

McCavity was falling, and the Doctor stuck his hand over the jet of escaping coolant gas. He felt the pain numb as the tissue froze, pulled his hand away before it was further damaged, and slammed it into the case. The glass shattered and flew.

'You've always liked sword fights, have you?' he said to his ice-flecked palm, checking the damage wasn't too great or the cuts too deep. 'You're a fighting hand, you are.' Then he grabbed the axe from within the shattered ice-like glass and yanked it free. He turned it, hefted it, brought it round in time to block McCavity's next blow.

And the next.

McCavity slashed and swung the sword at the Doctor, and each time the Doctor managed to block the blow. He made no attempt to attack McCavity. For one thing, the axe was too heavy and unwieldy – the blow would be so signposted that McCavity would easily be able to avoid it. Unless…

But McCavity was driving him back relentlessly. So the Doctor stepped sideways and aimed his own mighty blow. The axe swept down and hammered into its unmoving target. The cooling tank.

The head of the axe was buried in a sudden cloud of subfreezing steam, which jetted out, catching McCavity full in the face. He staggered away, arm over his eyes. But still he held on to his sword.

The Doctor wrenched the axe out of the rip in the tank and stepped warily towards his opponent, who was now doubled up, groaning. 'Come on,' the Doctor said, 'let's talk about this. We need to combine our forces, team up, play together to stop Salvo 7-50 and her gang, not fight each other. What do you say?'

McCavity straightened up. His face was cold and grey even in the red light. 'No chance!' he snarled, and swung the sword. But it was a pathetic attempt, with little strength behind it. The Doctor parried it easily – swinging the ice-coated axe into its path.

And the axe, cooled suddenly to well below freezing, shattered under the impact.

The Doctor staggered back in surprise, left holding the broken haft. Catching his foot on a cable, he crashed to the floor.

A figure seemed to rise up out of the cold red mist above the Doctor. McCavity raised the sword, his strength restored as his victim lay helpless in front of him. 'No chance,' he said again.

And he brought the sword slashing viciously down.

TEN

The sword stopped just shy of the Doctor's face. In the blood-red light, the Doctor could see that McCavity's hands were caught and held by huge black paws.

'You don't want to do that,' Kevin said. 'It's my job. Any idea of the problems you'll cause with the Monsters' Union if you go starting a demarcation dispute?'

The Doctor struggled to his feet. 'Look, why not take the Black Shadow off me?' he told McCavity. 'Then Kevin won't mind if you hack me to bits. Make 'em as small as you like.'

'Why don't I just let him finish the job?' McCavity shot back, pulling free of Kevin.

'Wait!'

The shout came from the back of the main engine room. Rose and Jimm were running towards them, splashing through spilled oil and coolant fluid. 'Wait!' Rose shouted again. 'Sally and the others'll be here in a minute. Dugg's holding them back as long as he can but...'

'They'll kill him,' Jimm said. He looked pale.

'That's his job,' McCavity said coldly.

'Daft,' Kevin sighed. 'But noble.'

'Talking of daft,' the Doctor said to McCavity, 'now you're in the mood to listen, maybe, I'm the only one who can get us out of here. So call Kevin off, or you'll be condemning yourself to death too.'

McCavity's eyes narrowed. He held up his hand to keep Kevin at bay.

Kevin sighed again. 'Kill him, don't kill him, kill him again. Just let me know when you finally make your tiny mind up, will you?'

'Whatever we're doing,' Rose said, 'let's do it quick.'

'Get the safety hatch at the end of the bulkhead shut,' the Doctor ordered, slapping the small piece of parchment into McCavity's hand. 'It won't keep them out for long, but it'll give us some time and they'll think we're trapped in here with no way out apart from the airlock and no spacesuits.'

'Whereas in fact,' Rose said hopefully, 'there *are* spacesuits?'

'Not that I've seen,' the Doctor told her.

'I'll get the hatch,' Kevin said. 'You just argue among yourselves for a bit and call if you need me or make your minds up or anything.'

'Oh, we need you,' the Doctor assured him. 'I'm hoping you don't actually need air.'

Jimm ran with Kevin to close the hatch.

'We managed to knock Cannon-K's head off with a

snooker ball,' Rose told the Doctor.

'Figures,' he said, apparently unimpressed. 'Action figures, in fact.' Then he grinned. 'That's really great, you know? Well done. Have a banana.'

'You what?' McCavity said in surprise.

'Neck's a weak point,' the Doctor said. 'If you'd had some decent toys and a well-adjusted childhood you might have known that.'

'Jimm did,' Rose agreed.

'Right then, air,' the Doctor announced as Kevin returned.

'Don't actually *need* it as such,' Kevin admitted. 'But it's nice to have. Bit of a luxury, I suppose. You know, like sudoku. Passes the time, but I can manage without if I have to. Actually,' he said thoughtfully, 'given the choice I'd probably take the sudoku. They're kind of addictive, aren't they? I keep meaning to get another book of them. Must talk to…' He stopped, shrugged, fixed the Doctor with his red eyes. 'What do you have in mind?'

The Doctor told them.

'You *are* joking,' McCavity said.

'I don't think he is,' Rose replied.

'If you think I'm carrying all four of you,' Kevin said, 'then you've got another thought coming. It'll mean two journeys at least.'

'Three,' the Doctor said. 'We still need the Resurrection Casket to bargain with.'

* * *

'That's better,' Cannon-K announced as Smithers finished the adjustments. He wiggled his head to check it was properly attached again. 'It's not much of a view from down there. But I did think I saw Polly.'

'Polly? I wouldn't have thought so,' Sally said. 'Old Poll must be long gone. I never understood why Glint needed a pet on board ship anyway. Just another thing to get in the way.'

'Maybe I was wrong,' Cannon-K admitted. 'Visual circuits were still a bit blurred. Seem fine now, though.'

'We're right on the edge of the zeg,' Smithers told him. 'Most systems will work. Probably just propulsion and navicomm that are all messed up.'

'Who's that?' Cannon-K asked, pointing at the body lying face down on the sofa.

'McCavity's man, whatever his name was,' Elvis said. 'Put up quite a fight. Not that it matters, they can't get out down there.'

'Only the engines,' Smithers agreed. 'There's the maintenance airlock, but no suits.'

'Cos we don't need 'em,' Sally said cheerfully, slapping her metal hand against Elvis's with a dull clang. 'Let's go and get the boss resurrected and kill us some ground-lubbers.'

She led the way down the corridor towards the engine rooms. 'Hey, Smithers, you remember the Vinitentian Marauders?'

'Thought they could outrun us,' Smithers recalled.

'But I fixed the trisilicate transfusion rate to boost the engines. That surprised them.'

'Scared them,' Elvis corrected him.

'Scared them to death,' Cannon-K said. And they all laughed.

They were still laughing when they reached the sealed hatchway that led into the main engine room.

'Getting a bit repetitive,' Sally said. 'Novelty's worn off rather. How are your hydraulics, Cannon-K?'

'Never better. Mind out.' Cannon-K flexed his arms, preparing to force open the door.

'Oh, give over,' Smithers said. 'That's my engine room in there. No one's keeping me out.'

'Uh-huh. Got an override code?' Elvis asked, impressed.

'Course I have.' Smithers flipped over a panel beside the hatch to reveal a keypad. He punched in a code. There was a click and the hatch swung slowly open.

'Nice one,' Sally said. Then she shouted through the hatch, 'Coming, ready or not!'

'There's no way out,' Smithers said confidently. 'We've got them now.'

It took them several minutes to search the engine room. Then they searched it again, just to be sure. After that they gathered beside a leaking cooling unit, looking at each other in robotic disbelief. The Doctor and his friends were gone.

His world was completely dark and absolutely silent

and Jimm was terrified. There was barely room to breathe, let alone move. He dared not cry out – not for fear of being heard but because it would use up the air.

The Doctor had told them all to breathe as shallowly as possible. Jimm wondered how the others were coping. After all, he was the smallest so he ought to have most room, yet the engineering locker seemed to fit tighter than his shoes. He could feel it jolting and bumping over the hull of the *Buccaneer* as Kevin dragged him and Rose in their separate, sealed containers to an airlock on the other side of the ship.

'Like being sealed in a microwave dinner,' Rose had said.

Jimm wasn't sure what that was – there were a lot of things that Rose and the Doctor said that he didn't understand – but he knew what she meant. When the Doctor had explained his plan he also mentioned that he wasn't sure if the lockers were in fact absolutely airtight but that they would soon discover. He seemed to find that as exciting and amusing as he found everything else.

The way they discovered was for Kevin to take the Doctor, sealed inside his own locker – waving cheerily as the lid closed over him – into the airlock and see if he was still alive inside after a couple of minutes. Rose had said that it didn't seem very scientific, and Jimm didn't think it seemed very safe. But the Doctor had protested it was pragmatic and the results would be empirical. Whatever that meant.

There was a final, bone-shaking jolt and Jimm's world settled into stillness as well as darkness and silence. The silence was broken by a knock on the lid.

'Anyone home?' The Doctor's voice was muffled but it was clear enough and Jimm found himself laughing. Then coughing as he used the last of the oxygen in his makeshift space pod. The lid opened and he gulped in the fresh air from outside. Close by he could see Rose sitting up inside her own locker. She was smiling, but she looked pale and Jimm guessed she had been every bit as spooked and afraid as he was.

'Where are we?' Rose wanted to know as the Doctor helped her out.

Kevin reached down and lifted Jimm easily from his own locker and stood him on his feet. 'You all right?' he asked, surprisingly gently.

'Fine, thanks.'

'Sorry it was a bit bumpy, but I thought it best to hurry.'

Jimm nodded. 'Thanks,' he said again.

'We're in the secondary control room,' the Doctor was saying. 'Closer than the main control deck and there's everything we need here.'

'Why, what are we going to do?' McCavity demanded. He was sitting in a pilot's chair and looked exhausted. His hair was plastered across his scalp with either sweat or liquid coolant. Or possibly a mixture of both.

'I'm going to turn everything back on,' the Doctor

said. 'As I thought. It looks as if there was a fairly orderly shutdown when the engines cut out. Probably a failsafe making sure the damage didn't spread. This ship was programmed to expect attack and possible catastrophic failure. So it shut down the non-essential systems. Probably why the life support and gravity are still working.'

'But won't turning it all back on again trigger a "catastrophic failure", then?' Rose said.

'Oh, that would be good. But sadly, I doubt it. Anything that was going to fail at this level of zeg interference will already have packed up big time.'

'So what is the point?' McCavity wanted to know.

'The point is,' the Doctor told him, 'that pretty soon Sally Salvo will realise we're not hiding in the engine room and will come looking for us again. And it won't take her long to guess where we're headed.'

'And where is that?'

'How about the only working spaceship in the area,' Rose said. 'Theirs. Or rather ours, before the mutiny.'

'So how does –' Jimm started to ask, but the Doctor cut him off.

'Let's just get on with it, shall we?' he said, not unkindly. 'Everything on. Turn every switch, push every lever, press every button and ford every stream. Follow every rainbow until…' He stopped, frowned, and said apologetically, 'Sorry, got a bit confused there. But you know what I mean. Right, main power cells.'

The lights dimmed slightly as the Doctor worked at the controls. Then the main lights flickered on – bright yellow blanket lighting.

'A good start,' the Doctor said with satisfaction. 'The cells are alive.'

'With the sound of music?' Rose suggested.

They were running, Sally leading the way.

'Main control deck,' Smithers said. 'That's where they'll be.'

'Not any more,' Elvis grated. 'They'll be heading for the ship.'

'Less talk, more speed,' Sally shouted. In her opinion the Doctor and the others would have used the secondary control suite. It was closer to the docked steamship, so they could get away more quickly. But that didn't answer the most important question. 'Smithers,' she called back, 'why have they restored power and onlined the systems?'

'Something they need?' Cannon-K suggested.

'We'll ask them,' Elvis said. 'Before we kill them.'

'What if they undock before we reach them?' Smithers asked.

'Then we shoot them out of the sky with the *Buccaneer*'s electro-blasters,' Sally replied. 'Since the Doctor's been kind enough to bring them back online.'

'That'll leave us stranded here,' Smithers pointed out.

'Be fun, though,' Elvis told him.

Sally was slowing, steam puffing erratically from her joints. 'Go on,' she said to the others. 'Stop them. Keep their ship here. I need a top-up. I'll get some water from the galley on seventh deck.'

'So now what?' Rose asked.

They were back on the ship, and Kevin had swung the heavy docking hatch closed and locked it.

'We leave,' McCavity said. 'Right now.'

'Actually,' the Doctor told them, 'no. We don't.'

'Why not?' Jimm asked.

'Because as soon as we're clear of the *Buccaneer*, they'll shoot us down. It'll leave them stranded, but then they'd be stranded if we left anyway. Spite's a pretty powerful emotion, you know. They'd shoot us down without a qualm.'

'That's because you onlined the systems,' McCavity snapped.

'Yes,' the Doctor snapped back. 'It is. And I did it for a good reason. Control deck. Now.' He spun on his heel and led the way.

'Bring that,' McCavity told Kevin, pointing to the black casket. He lifted his space chest and carried it after the Doctor, Rose and Jimm.

'Your word is my command, O Smell in the Wind,' Kevin muttered.

Smithers had removed an access panel by the docking

bay and was sorting through a mass of cables and wires.

'Hurry up,' Elvis said. 'They'll be undocking any moment unless you can break the servo linkage.'

'Yeah, that'll surprise them,' Cannon-K agreed.

'Only if he's quick. Otherwise they'll be long gone and we'll be stranded.'

Sally hurried to join them. 'Sorry about that, it took a minute for the water to reach boiling. I nearly seized up completely.' She watched Smithers for a moment. 'So they're in the ship?'

'Yes.'

'But they haven't undocked.'

'No.'

'And you're trying to –'

'Trying to make sure they don't. Yes.' He had two wires held in his metal fingers. 'Now, is it red or yellow?' he wondered.

'So why haven't they left?' Elvis wondered. 'What are they waiting for?'

A view screen flickered into life close to where Smithers was working. The Doctor's pixellated face grinned out at them, broken by occasional flashes of static. 'I expect you're wondering why we haven't left,' he said.

'Never crossed our minds,' Sally told him.

'No? Oh well, never mind. You've probably managed to isolate the servo linkages so we can't undock anyway. And if you haven't, it's the yellow wire you want.'

'Thanks,' Smithers said quietly. He snapped the wire.

'Or possibly the red one,' the Doctor continued. 'I can never remember. Still, we know that if we try to leave you'll just blow us out of space for the hell of it anyway. So I propose a deal.'

'A deal?' Sally made it sound like something slimy and unpleasant. 'What deal?'

'Simple. You let us go back to Starfall and we nudge the *Buccaneer* out of the zeg for you. You don't follow us. Well, you couldn't, could you? You'd be zegged again. What do you say? That way everyone lives, which is something I'm always in favour of.'

'Everyone except Glint,' Sally told him.

'Except Glint,' the Doctor agreed. 'We have the Resurrection Casket and we're keeping it. So – deal?'

Sally looked at her crewmates. 'I'm not quite sure how this is a good deal for us,' she said slowly. 'It sounds like, you leave us here without what we came for and in return we agree not to kill you all.'

'Sounds like it, yeah.'

'Whereas, since you can't undock, we could decide instead to break down the hatch, take what we want and kill you all anyway. Then we'll have the casket, Glint and a working steamship we can use to push the *Buccaneer* out of the zeg.'

'Yeah, well, I guess that's true. But what about honour among thieves and the pirate code and nobility and generosity and mercy and goodwill to all life forms?'

'We don't subscribe to any of those, do we?' Sally asked quietly.

The others shook their heads.

'Don't think so,' Elvis said.

'No,' Cannon-K agreed.

'Definitely not,' Smithers added.

'Sorry, Doctor,' Sally said to the screen. 'Not our sort of thing really. We're more into death and destruction.'

The Doctor was nodding. He looked sad but resigned. 'OK, let me put it this way, then. We nudge your ship out of the zeg and then you let us go. Or I'll destroy you. You'll all die. Quite horribly. That work for you?'

Cannon-K was laughing – great rasping, throaty metallic roars of amusement. 'Oh, let's kill them all now,' he said.

The Doctor's expression was anything but amused. 'Last chance. I can kill you all any time I want. Now, what's your decision?'

Sally, Elvis and Smithers looked at each other. For the first time, they felt the slightest edge of fear.

But Cannon-K was still laughing. 'Prove it,' he roared.

'If I must.'

'Oh, you must!'

Half of Sally's face was frowning. Her mind was going over the situation again and again – had she missed something or was he bluffing? He had to be bluffing. She barely heard the Doctor's words to Cannon-K.

'I've written down exactly how I'm going to do it,' he was saying. 'It's on a piece of paper Mr McCavity left below the hatchway. You see it?'

'Oh yeah. Here it is.' Cannon-K went to the hatch and bent to pick up the paper.

Sally's mind cleared as she realised what the Doctor had said. 'Wait – stop!'

But it was too late. Cannon-K had picked up the scrap of paper. He unfolded it. He stared at the blotchy dark shape drawn on it. The Black Shadow. And a darkness fell across him as something faded into existence between the robot and the main lighting.

'Poll?' Cannon-K said. His mechanical voice seemed to tremble.

'Sorry about this,' Kevin said. 'And if you want to talk to me in future, call me by my real name. Don't *ever* call me Poll again.' He reached for the point where Cannon-K's heavy head precariously joined his shoulders. 'Though I don't think that'll be a problem.'

They watched on the monitor with a sort of horrified fascination.

'Why don't you rip them all to bits for us?' Jimm asked as Kevin faded back into solid form beside them.

'Doesn't work like that. I can't, not without specific instructions.'

'The Black Shadow.'

'That's right.'

'Can't you just help us out?' Rose asked.

Kevin shook his head. 'Sorry. I step out of line and I get a free long holiday to somewhere south of heaven. Not acceptable.'

On the screen Sally was staring in fury and disbelief at the scattered components and bent metal that had been Cannon-K. 'I'll kill you for this, Poll!' she shouted. 'You jumped-up ship's parrot! You wait – I'll rip the medallion from that human's fragile neck before I kill him and then I'll see you burn in Hades for all eternity.'

'Don't call me Poll,' Kevin said angrily.

But Sally had already turned away. 'Don't touch anything,' she was telling Elvis and Smithers. 'Pick up nothing made of paper, nothing that could have paper in it or attached to it or glued underneath it, understand – nothing!' She turned back to the screen. 'I'll kill you all for this,' she said. 'And that's a promise.'

'You've already heard my promise,' the Doctor said quietly. 'Last chance. *Really* last chance.'

'You're bluffing,' Sally said. 'Break down the hatch.'

The massive boilers of the steamship *Venture* were working at full pressure. Flow valves opened and steam jetted along the pipes to the main thrust outlets.

Slowly at first, having to carry the huge weight of the *Buccaneer* as well as its own mass, the *Venture* started to move. Struggling and straining, it gently eased forwards, pushing the enormous bulk of the larger ship ahead of it…

Sally, Elvis and Smithers all felt the slight jolt as the ship shuddered and started to move. Elvis and Smithers were working at the hatch, tearing at the backs of the rivets holding the locking mechanism.

'They're trying to break free,' Smithers said.

'No,' Sally said. 'They haven't so much as attempted to disengage the clamps. Does he think that if he moves us out of the zeg we'll just let them go?'

'Going the wrong way for that,' Smithers said without looking up. 'My motion sensors put us on a course of two seven nine by five one four. That's taking us further into the zeg.'

He stopped working at a rivet and slowly stood up. 'Oh, my cripes,' he said.

Then Smithers and Elvis were running, racing as fast as they could back towards the engineering section.

Sally went to the screen. Lines of interference were shooting across it, but the Doctor's face was still visible through the increasing blizzard.

'Very clever,' Sally shouted. 'But it won't work. Smithers and Elvis will offline and revert to steam operation. And the zeg doesn't affect me anyway. You won't kill me that easily.'

For a moment the screen cleared and she could see the Doctor talking to the others. They seemed to be preparing to leave.

'I'm not trying to kill you,' the Doctor said, turning back to the screen. 'I don't have to.' Then he turned away again, as if she was no longer of any consequence. 'Right,' he was shouting to his friends, 'we need to get to the forward escape pod before...' Then his voice was lost in white noise and static. The picture became a mass of grey.

Sally stared at the useless screen. What did he mean? Somewhere deep in the *Buccaneer* there was an explosion. Then another. The ship began to tremble and shake, and suddenly Sally realised. She turned and stumbled across the shaking deck, heading for the nearest airlock.

The *Venture* itself was unaffected. But Rose could feel the jolting, hear the muffled explosions as the *Buccaneer*'s systems failed. If they stayed attached to the large ship, then it was only a matter of time before they got damaged.

Jimm was holding on to a control panel, McCavity clutching hold of the other side of it. Rose was leaning against the wall, hoping she wouldn't lose her balance. It was like being on a really rickety tube train as it shuddered out of the station.

Kevin seemed to have little difficulty keeping upright, his large feet planted well apart and his massive arms folded. He looked bored with the whole thing. Which was a contrast to the Doctor, who was staggering backwards and forwards as the pod shook, laughing gleefully and treating the whole thing like a fairground ride.

'We'll be torn apart if we don't disengage!' McCavity shouted over the increasing sound of vibration and distant explosions.

The Doctor managed to stay still for long enough to frown. 'Do you think so?' Then he was hurled against the wall close to Rose, bounced off and landed on his back on the floor. 'Could have a point actually,' he admitted. 'But we can't disengage, Sally's got us locked in place.'

'So there's no escape?' Jimm said, still clinging tightly to the console.

'Oh, I didn't say that. We're quite safe, aren't we, Rose?' The Doctor leaped to his feet. 'Twice as safe. This way, come on.' And he staggered and swayed out of the room.

Elvis was struggling to connect his breastplate. Smithers had been quicker – he was an engineer. He already had his plates back in place and was tightening the last few screws.

'Help me, will you?' Elvis croaked.

The whole ship was creaking and shaking, as if in a storm.

'I need to offline,' Smithers grated. 'Losing speech and motive power...' His voice faded and he stood absolutely still. Waiting for the water in his systems to reach boiling point.

Elvis too was frozen in position. His hand shuddered as he tried desperately to move it, to make the last few connections.

But as the ship heaved and buckled he realised it would do no good. The systems the Doctor had brought back online were now failing catastrophically. The main drive units were breaking up. The hull was being ripped apart as the fuel lines and control linkages built into its very fabric fractured and exploded.

The *Buccaneer* was tearing itself apart around them.

'Why am I the only one without a box?' Jimm wanted to know. 'McCavity has his chest, Kevin's got the casket, and now you two have that blue box.'

The escape pod was identical to the one they had used to reach the *Buccaneer*, except for the large blue box standing in the middle of it. The Doctor patted the side of the box affectionately. 'Locked us out again,' he said. 'Still, once we head back out of the zeg we should be OK.'

'And what about Sally and the others?' Rose asked.

'Yes, a clever plan,' McCavity conceded. 'But you heard Sally. She's not affected by the zeg. What's to stop her coming after us?'

'Assuming she escapes that?' the Doctor asked, pointing to the porthole.

Outside, as the pod detached from the *Venture* and floated gently away, the whole of the *Buccaneer* was coming apart. Debris battered against the outside of the pod, clanging and crashing as it ricocheted past.

'Look, there's Elvis,' Jimm said, pointing. 'And Smithers.'

The two robots were twisting and turning in among the debris. Elvis seemed rigid as a statue as he floated clear of the ship. But Smithers was heading straight for the pod, propelled by bursts of steam from his legs.

'Ah, we don't need to worry about them,' the Doctor announced.

'Oh?' Rose said. 'Don't we?'

'No. We can leave them to the local wildlife.'

As he spoke a huge krark appeared from behind the pod, launching itself past the porthole and powering into Smithers, driving the robot back towards the wreckage.

'Dinner time,' the Doctor said quietly. 'Well, that's that, then.'

'Not quite,' McCavity said. 'I gave you an ultimatum, Doctor, and it still stands. Operate the Resurrection Casket for me, bring back Larissa, or you die.'

The Doctor sighed. 'And I told you. It's not possible. It wasn't possible back on the ship and it still isn't possible here. Look, you have to let her go. Let her rest in peace. And when we get back to Starfall you can account for your crimes to the proper authorities.'

'Oh, can I?'

'Yes. You can and you will. I made Silver Sally a promise and I kept it. Now I'm making you one. You will own up to your responsibilities and to what you have done. There's a price that needs to be paid, and believe me you'll pay it.'

But McCavity just laughed. 'Oh, listen to you, the high and mighty Doctor. The high and mighty *dead* Doctor.'

'Oh, not that Black Shadow nonsense again? I won't let you pass me a cursed piece of paper this time, you know.'

'No?' Somehow he seemed to find that even more funny.

'Excuse me, Doctor,' Kevin said, stepping out from behind the TARDIS. 'But I think you'll find he's already put it in your coat pocket. Sorry.'

ELEVEN

The Doctor ducked out of the way of Kevin's paws. 'Take your time,' he said. 'No rush. I'm not going anywhere, after all.' He nipped quickly round the TARDIS, aiming to keep it between himself and Kevin.

Rose and Jimm ran to Kevin, trying to hold him back. But he gently yet firmly moved Rose aside. Jimm held on to the creature's fur, tugging and pulling. Kevin ignored him, lumbering after the Doctor round the TARDIS.

In desperation, Rose went for McCavity instead. 'Call him off,' she demanded. But McCavity backhanded her viciously across the face, sending her sprawling against the airlock door.

'Keep out of this, girlie,' McCavity hissed. 'Or you'll be next.'

'Girlie?' Rose struggled to her feet. 'Girlies fight dirty with nails and teeth and kicking.' She glared at McCavity, and he took a step backwards, suddenly worried by what he saw in her expression. 'So maybe you're right. We'll see.'

The Doctor appeared round the TARDIS. 'You show him, girlie,' he said with a grin. Then the grin disappeared, and so did the Doctor, as Kevin lunged for him.

'Just trying to do my job,' the monster muttered in irritation. 'Then I can go home and put my feet up for a bit. I was halfway through a crossword, you know.'

'What's the clue you're stuck on?' the Doctor's voice asked from the other side of the TARDIS.

Jimm was still clinging to Kevin as the monster charged round the TARDIS in pursuit of the Doctor. '"I'll buy you a new pair of trousers, says playwright",' Kevin told him.

'I'll need more than new trousers,' the Doctor retorted.

'No, that's the clue. Nine letters. It's eleven down, if that helps.'

Rose was advancing slowly on McCavity. She wasn't really sure what she was going to do, but one option was to rip his arms off and beat him with the yucky ends until he called Kevin off.

'Airlock!' Jimm cried as Kevin shook him free and he went careering across the pod. He slammed into the wall and stumbled back, dazed.

'That's only seven letters,' Kevin said.

'No...' Jimm was rubbing his head. 'There's someone in the airlock.'

He was right. Rose could hear the hiss of air as the antechamber pressurised.

'Don't let her in!' the Doctor shouted.

'Who?' Rose said.

The Doctor's face appeared for a moment before he ducked out of sight again. 'Who do you think? Your mum?!'

Through the thick glass porthole, Rose could see Silver Sally patiently waiting for the pressure to equalise and the door to open. Behind her, through the outer door, Rose could see a krark circling hopefully.

'Let me in!' Sally's voice was surprisingly clear – coming through an intercom grille beside the door.

McCavity turned a locking lever, just as the hiss of air stopped. The door shuddered as Sally tried to force it open. But it held firm. The krark smacked into the outer door, its blunt nose smearing across the porthole and making the whole pod shudder.

'Let me in!' Sally pleaded again. 'Please let me in!'

'No chance,' McCavity told her.

'So now what?' the Doctor shouted across the pod. He was busily dancing from side to side to evade Kevin's paws. Either the creature was slower than him or it was giving him a sporting chance.

'You know what it is?' Kevin demanded.

'What, your crossword answer? Course I do.'

'Well?'

'If I tell you, will you let me go?'

'No.'

'Thought not.'

'So you might as well tell me anyway.'

'Oh, come on!' The Doctor dived to one side, rolled, leaped to his feet and ducked behind the TARDIS again.

'At least give me a clue,' Kevin pleaded.

'You've got a clue.'

'Very funny.'

'It's all Greek to me,' the Doctor shouted back.

'Is that a clue?'

'What do you think?'

Sally was hammering on the door now. Behind her, the glass of the outer porthole cracked as the krark slammed into it again.

'Don't let her in,' McCavity insisted.

'Like I'd listen to you,' Rose told him.

She looked at Sally through the glass. And as well as a metallic, inhuman killer, she saw the fear and the humanity of the other side of Sally – the frightened little girl who stared back at her from one side of Sally's jigsaw face. Was any of that real girl left? Could Rose condemn her to death too?

'Please,' Sally mouthed. 'Please let me in.' Her hand – her human hand – pressed palm-flat against the glass, and Rose was surprised how small it was.

She looked for help, and found that McCavity was gone. He had turned away to watch the final encounter between Kevin and the Doctor. Jimm was standing beside Rose now, staring at the hand on the porthole.

McCavity turned and looked back at Rose. 'The red

lever,' he said. 'Pull it to the left.'

But Jimm was furiously shaking his head. 'That's the outer door. That'll shoot her out into space and the krarks will get her.'

'That's right,' McCavity shouted back. 'That's what she deserves.'

Rose almost pulled the lever. Almost. He was right. It was what she deserved. 'And what do you deserve?' Rose shouted at McCavity. 'She's not the only killer round here, you know.'

'OK, OK,' the Doctor was standing clear of the TARDIS with his hands up in a gesture of surrender. 'We can't go on like this all day.'

Kevin approached him warily.

'You'll bring back Larissa?' McCavity said eagerly.

'I can't,' the Doctor told him. There was real sadness in his eyes. 'Really, I can't. So let me just say goodbye.' He looked over to the airlock, meeting Rose's eyes. 'Rose – it's been fun. Do whatever you think best. You're not wrong. You're never wrong. How could you be?'

She blinked back the tears and reached for the lever that McCavity had used to lock the inner airlock door. It moved easily and the door swung open. 'No tricks, all right?' Rose told her as Sally all but fell into the pod. Rose pulled the door shut behind her.

'Thank you,' Sally gasped.

Rose pointed at her – finger under the girl's half-chin. 'Not another word,' she said.

Kevin stood, hands on hips, watching as the Doctor shook hands seriously with Jimm.

'Oh, get on with it,' McCavity said, looking warily from the Doctor to Sally and back again.

'Jimm,' the Doctor was saying, still holding his hand, 'you know what to do too, don't you?'

'Yes, Doctor. I know.'

'Good lad.'

As soon as Jimm stepped aside, Kevin took his place. The Doctor shook his paw. 'No hard feelings,' he said. 'Got the answer yet? Did you think Greek?'

Kevin's chest heaved in a gasp of realisation. 'Of course. Thanks, Doctor. "Euripides", right?'

'You got it. Now just give me a moment, will you?'

'Why?' McCavity demanded. 'Get on with it. I'm going to enjoy this.'

But the smile disappeared from his face as Jimm launched himself at the man, driving him back against the pod wall in fury.

'You murderer!' Jimm yelled. 'You killed your wife, and Kaspar and Ronny and the others, and now you're going to kill the Doctor. I won't let you do it!'

McCavity flung him aside and pulled himself back to his feet, eyes blazing. 'You're next!' he spat.

'Excuse me!' the Doctor shouted back at him. 'I'm trying to say what might be my last words here, so no interruptions please. Now I made Sally there a promise earlier. And I've kept it. I make you a promise too, McCavity. Either you let me go, either you annul the Black Shadow and call Kevin off, or I promise you will regret it.'

'Regret it?' McCavity gave a roar of laughter. 'Not for one moment, Doctor. The Black Shadow stays. Irrevocable. Until my Being of Darkness has done its work.'

'You won't change your mind?' the Doctor asked sadly. He pulled a piece of paper from his pocket and unfolded it. He held it so that McCavity could see clearly the dark smudge of ink that condemned the Doctor to death. 'You won't ever release Kevin from his duty, no matter what happens?'

'Never.' McCavity was staring at the paper. He licked his lips in anticipation. 'Whatever happens, Creature of the Night, you will perform this solemn task for me.'

'Creature of the Night,' Kevin muttered. 'Being of Darkness. Crikey O'Reilly, you're full of it, aren't you?'

'Just do it!' McCavity shouted. 'Now!'

'If you insist.' Kevin raised his massive paws, turned and lumbered menacingly forwards. But not towards the Doctor. Towards McCavity.

'What are you doing?' McCavity backed away. 'I gave you an instruction. Clear and irreversible.'

'I know.' Still Kevin was coming towards him.

'It's the Doctor you must kill, you fool,' McCavity yelled. He stumbled and almost fell, tripping on the black shape of the Resurrection Casket left against the pod wall. 'He is holding the Black Shadow.'

The massive creature paused, turned back towards the Doctor. The Doctor held up the piece of paper cheerfully for them all to see.

Kevin shook his head. 'He's holding a piece of paper,' he growled, 'that says the Black Shadow is in your pocket.'

'What!' McCavity's eyes widened, as if what he could see on the paper was changing even as he looked at it. He fumbled in his pocket and pulled out a piece of paper that was almost identical. The middle of it was stained with an inky black shape.

'Well done, Jimm. Psychic paper, this,' the Doctor explained. 'It shows you what I want you to see. Or in this case, what you expected to see. Probably that's cheating,' he admitted. 'But – what the hell.'

'Irreversible, you said,' Kevin told McCavity as he continued to advance on him. 'You know, usually at this point I apologise. Seems only fair. But this time I don't think I'll bother.'

'Stop,' McCavity was screaming. 'I order you. By the power of…' He tore at the chain round his neck, but it was broken and fell away.

Across on the other side of the pod, Jim held up the gold medallion he had pulled from McCavity's throat as they fought.

McCavity was looking round, desperately searching for an escape. But there was none. Kevin loomed up in front of him. The wall was behind him. At his feet was the Resurrection Casket. He fell to his knees, scrabbling at the lid of the casket.

'Er, I wouldn't open that,' the Doctor said.

'Stop him,' Rose yelled. 'He'll release Glint!'

'At last!' Sally said beside her.

Rose felt the hot steam of Sally's breath against her cheek. But she could not turn, could not look away as McCavity finally managed to unlock the lid and open the casket.

'Don't open it,' the Doctor was saying again. 'Because if you do…'

The lid was wide open now. McCavity stared into the casket. Kevin leaned forward.

'I don't believe it,' McCavity whispered.

'Because, if you do, you'll find,' the Doctor said quietly, 'that the casket is empty.'

McCavity leaped to his feet, spinning round to stare at the Doctor. 'It's a fake. This isn't the casket.'

'Oh yes, it is.'

'Then it doesn't work.' McCavity took a step back as Kevin reached for him. His feet caught on the casket behind him and he fell backwards into it with a cry of surprise. Kevin hesitated and Jimm raced past, slamming the lid down and cutting off McCavity's wails of fear and anger. He held up the medallion.

'I'm the boss now,' Jimm said. 'Leave him in there.'

'I can't do that,' Kevin said.

'I think you can.' The Doctor had joined them, looking down at the plain black casket. 'After all, you know as well as I do that what's in there isn't really

Drel McCavity any more. Not the McCavity that murdered and killed and cheated and lied. Maybe it'll come to that, but not…' His voice tailed off as he looked across the pod, and saw Rose and Sally.

Standing just inside the airlock door.

Rose's face was pale and her eyes were wide and moist.

Sally's metal hand was clamped tight round Rose's throat, tiny breaths of steam escaping from the knuckles and the wrist as she tightened her grip.

TWELVE

Rose had to struggle to speak. Her throat felt like it was being squeezed tight closed and she could barely breathe. 'I trusted you,' she managed to gasp. 'I trusted you *again*.'

'And how stupid is that?' Sally said. The side of her face that could actually show an expression was looking at Rose with complete contempt. 'That's why I'm tougher than you. That's why I'm a survivor.'

The Doctor and Jim were edging closer.

'Don't do anything rash,' the Doctor warned Sally.

'She's my bargaining chip. I'm not going to kill her,' Sally assured him. 'Not so long as you do what I tell you.'

'And what's that? What do you want?' Jimm asked.

Kevin was padding slowly towards Sally, but she turned, so that Rose's body was between them. 'Don't even think about it, Poll,' she spat. 'I know what'll happen to you if you kill when you weren't ordered to, without the Black Shadow. And if anyone tries to get the Black Shadow on me, I'll kill Rose as sure as krarks are krarks.'

Kevin stopped. He was shaking with anger, but even through her misty eyes, Rose could tell he was not going to be any help. 'Why d'you call him Poll?' she managed to ask.

Sally found that funny. Thin jets of steam escaped from the metal side of her face in time to the laughter. 'It's a nickname. Short for Polly.'

'Polly?' Jimm said.

'As in Polly Parrot, yes?' the Doctor said.

'That's right,' Kevin said angrily. 'It was a long time ago. No one calls me Poll now.'

'Polly Parrot,' Sally said, mimicking a parrot, still laughing. 'The ship's parrot, captain's pet monster. No use at all. Just a tame monster who's allowed out every now and again when there's a job to be done that no one else can be bothered with.'

'Killing people,' the Doctor said, the disgust evident in his voice.

'Or cleaning the latrines,' Sally said. 'Scrubbing the aft decks. Ironing the captain's shirts. We got Poll – sorry, *Kevin* – to do all the really interesting jobs for us.'

Kevin was shaking with fury. 'Who's the steam iron now?' he demanded. 'Huh? Who's reduced to holding girls hostage to get what they want? I bet you'd have never got eleven down even with the Doctor's help. Silver Sally, is it? Silly Sally more like.'

'Children,' the Doctor admonished.

But Kevin was into his stride now. 'Silly Sally, silly Sally, silly Sally,' he sang in his gruff voice.

'Shut up!' Sally shouted at him.

'All she can do is shilly-shally. Silly Sally, shilly-shally.'

'Shut up! Shut up or I kill her.'

'Quiet!' Jimm ordered, holding up the medallion for Kevin to see.

'It's just a song,' the disgruntled Kevin said. He kicked his heels and looked fed up. 'Can't even sing a song now.'

'Doctor – please,' Rose croaked, struggling to stand more upright and get some air into her lungs. She didn't need to move much. Just enough to be able to shift her weight on to her left leg, to raise her right foot...

'Yes, sorry. So, what's the deal here, then?' the Doctor asked Sally.

'The deal is that I'm going back to Starfall. In this pod. Just me – and Hamlek Glint. Listening now?'

'But Glint's dead. He's gone,' Rose managed to say. Almost there now, almost there...

'Don't be so stupid,' Sally told her. She relaxed her grip slightly, perhaps believing now that Rose was no threat at all.

'And what about the rest of us?'

'If you're good I'll drop you off on a ship somewhere. One with life support. If you're lucky.'

'And we just wait there and hope to be rescued?'

'That's right.'

'And if we say no?' Jimm asked.

'You really don't have any choice,' Sally told them, pulling Rose closer to her.

'Oh, there's always a choice,' the Doctor replied calmly. 'It's just a question of working out what the options are. OK, Rose,' he added in the same tone of voice. 'When you're ready. She's all yours, girlie.'

Rose slammed her right heel down on Sally's human ankle. The pirate girl's grip on Rose's throat slackened in surprise, just enough for Rose to wrench herself free. She kicked, hard, at the ankle again.

Sally collapsed, down on one knee. She looked up at Rose in anger and surprise. A second later, the Doctor was grinning down at her. He was holding his sonic screwdriver and the end was glowing a faint blue.

'Now, here's the new deal,' he said. 'And either you can agree or I can increase the resonance of my sonic screwdriver and boil away the water in your systems so that half of you at least will seize up so tight it'll never move again. Listening now?'

'So, you finally worked it out, did you?' the Doctor asked Sally.

She was sitting on the floor with her back against the pod wall. The Doctor was sitting close by, cross-legged with his sonic screwdriver aimed. He had told her he could vaporise the water in her joints and boilers in less than a second, though Rose reckoned he was bluffing. Hopefully, she wouldn't have to find out.

'About Glint and the treasure?' Sally said. One side of her face was sulking.

'I haven't,' Rose said. 'What about you, Jimm?' The boy shook his head. 'So tell us. And why was the casket empty?'

'Shouldn't we let Mr McCavity out?' Jimm asked.

'He's fine where he is,' the Doctor said. 'We'll check on him in a bit.'

'And Glint?' Jimm said.

'You really don't know?' Sally said.

'One more word,' the Doctor said in a very reasonable tone, 'and it's bye-bye, movement. Got it?'

Sally opened her mouth. Then she closed it again without answering. Instead, she nodded.

'Now, pretty soon we'll be at the edge of the zeg and we'll find a nice escape pod, like ours only with all mod cons and everything. We'll dump you in that and you can make your way to wherever you wish to go. And if you ever try to come back to Starfall or I ever see you again…' He brandished the sonic screwdriver. 'Well, I'll leave that to your imagination, such as it is.'

The Doctor settled himself comfortably and patted the floor beside him, encouraging Rose and Jimm to sit down. Kevin stayed where he was, leaning against the TARDIS with his massive hairy arms folded, staring down at Sally with what looked like a grin on his shaggy face.

'Let me tell you a story,' the Doctor said. 'I'm pretty sure it's a true story, but I don't want any interruptions even if it isn't.'

He paused to glare meaningfully at Sally. She held his gaze for a moment, then looked at the floor.

'It's a story all about pirates,' the Doctor went on. 'And it starts once upon a time about fifty years ago, when a dangerous and nasty pirate called Hamlek Glint decided to pack it all in. Maybe he'd had enough, or maybe he just fancied a change. I'd like to think that he became a pirate by accident somehow – forced into it by circumstances. Maybe he never intended to kill and hurt so very many people. Maybe he was egged on by his cut-throat robot crew and finally managed to cut loose and get rid of them and pack it all in. But that's probably just wishful thinking on my part. Who knows?'

'Seems you do,' Kevin said. 'Go on.'

'Well, this pirate, this Captain Glint bloke, managed to trick his robot crew and abandon them. Sold them for scrap, though as we now know some of them managed to escape their pressing engagement and came looking for him. Not for revenge, but because they missed the good old days of blood and thunder and wanted to re-create their misspent youths. Only

Glint was long gone by then. I mean, this was fifty years ago. They were looking for him for a very long time.

'And in that time,' the Doctor continued, 'a few things had happened. For one, Glint's cabin boy Robbie left him too. I think he'd had enough as well. I think he'd realised that a life in the spaceways wasn't as romantic and exciting as it was cracked up to be. There were death and blood and suffering. So when Glint climbed into the Resurrection Casket, expecting to be reborn anew, Robbie legged it. Not literally of course. He took an escape pod and left the *Buccaneer* drifting in space.'

'But the casket was empty,' Rose pointed out.

The Doctor nodded. 'Coming to that,' he promised. 'So Robbie takes the pod – and the treasure – and off he goes, shutting down all the systems first so Glint can't come after him without powering up first. Only with no crew the ship's drifted into the zeg, which no one really knew much about back then. So Glint's stranded, and Robbie is stuck in a pod he can't control. It just flies on in a straight line, taking him and the treasure to… Well, who knows where?'

'And Kevin?' Jimm wanted to know. 'What happened to him?'

'Oh, Kevin is sitting snug at home with a mug of tea or whatever, wherever home is, waiting for orders and quite happy if they never come. After all, he just wants to be free of it all, don't you, my friend?'

'You can say that again,' Kevin agreed.

'But something happens to prevent that. Ten years ago, give or take, the medallion that controls Kevin comes into the possession of some reprobates who sell it to Drel McCavity. Now, here's a man who has suddenly become interested in Glint, partly because he needs a new obsession now his wife has gone, and partly as a reason for him to have on display a particularly nasty sculpture that isn't at all what it seems. After all, the poor man's subordinates are probably hunting high and low for him, though they'd never think to search McCavity's house after what's apparently happened. But whether McCavity got the medallion before or after he killed his unfaithful wife in a fit of pique really makes no odds. He's rather surprised to find he has a monster – no offence – at his beck and call. And while he uses Kevin sparingly, at first, he does have a bit of a temper, doesn't he?'

'So what happened to Glint?' Rose said. 'From that story, he should still be in the casket.'

'Well, I think Kevin knows.'

They all looked up at Kevin, except for the Doctor, who had not taken his eyes off Sally.

'Like the Doctor said,' Kevin told them, 'once McCavity hauled me back to this dimension I had a lot of time on my hands between jobs. I spent some of it on Starfall and a lot of it back on the *Buccaneer*. Can't say I ever really liked it, and the company was dreadful, but it was home of a sort.'

'And you found Robbie, didn't you?'

'Sure did. Poor kid was all cut up with guilt about leaving Glint. I tried to tell him, but he knew all about the zeg by then and thought he'd left Glint to die. So…' Kevin shrugged. 'I gave him the coordinates of the ship and he came back in a steam cutter, oh, must be about ten years ago now, and he opened the casket.'

'He let Glint out?' Jimm said.

'Yes,' Kevin said. 'He did. And took him back with him.'

'You released Glint?' Rose said. 'But why?'

'Because Robbie was my friend, that's why. The only friend I had in those awful days. The only one who even called me by my real name. That's why. And I'd do it again.'

There was silence for a while, then the Doctor pulled himself suddenly to his feet. 'Here,' he said to Rose, 'hold this.' He handed her the sonic screwdriver. 'I should think we're almost out of the zeg now, so let's see if I can find a suitable container for our chum Salvage Sally here. Doesn't have to be much – just enough to keep out the kraks and let her steer a course well away from us.'

The pod was from an old Dressonian freighter. It was pockmarked with meteorite scars and the main observation window was cracked. But it still had an atmosphere and rudimentary propulsion based on gas turbines.

'No moving parts,' the Doctor said. 'All solid-state compressed gas rather than steam. But the zeg shouldn't even interfere with the engines, which is the main thing. You'll be all right. Just head off towards civilisation and out of the zone and you'll get picked up. Eventually.'

Sally glared at him through her one good eye.

'Remember,' the Doctor said quietly as she got into the pod, 'there's always a choice. Make the right one just this once, why don't you?'

The robot-girl did not reply. The Doctor closed the hatch and spun the locking wheel.

'Not our problem any more then, is that it?' Rose asked.

'It's all down to choices,' the Doctor said.

'But after what she's done. You're just letting her go. She's stolen someone's *face*, Doctor. She's killed people.'

'And you let her into the pod, remember.'

'Yeah, but she'd have died.'

The Doctor shrugged. 'She's just a robot, despite all the personality and emotion programming. But you took pity on her. You gave her a choice, even though she plumped for the wrong option. Don't give me grief for doing the same thing.'

'I think it's wrong,' she told him.

'It's my choice,' he replied. 'And hers. Though I

don't think it's in her nature to choose the right option.'

He pulled a lever on the main control panel in their own pod and Sally's broke free.

They watched Sally's pod drifting away from them. For a few moments her face was clearly visible at the observation window, the crack in the glass like the split in her face. The Doctor waved. Sally did not wave back.

'So, it's goodbye time,' the Doctor said. 'Time we were off while the TARDIS is still working. We'll set you on a course back to Starfall, Jimm.'

'We're leaving him on his own?' Rose asked.

'I can manage,' Jimm insisted.

'Kevin can help,' the Doctor said. 'Jimm's got the medallion.'

'That's right,' Jimm remembered, and pulled it from his pocket. 'Only…'

'Yes?' The Doctor sounded hopeful, and Rose wondered what he was up to now.

'Kevin wants his freedom. He doesn't want to have to do what I tell him.'

The huge hairy creature looked down kindly at the boy. 'I've been doing it for long enough,' he said. 'Another few days while we get back to Starfall won't matter much. Or weeks, or months. Or even years, come to that.'

'No,' Jimm said. 'No, you should help because you want to, not because you have to.'

He handed Kevin the medallion.

The gold disc was almost lost in the monster's enormous paw. He looked down at it through blood-red eyes that seemed to glow with moisture.

'Thank you,' Kevin said quietly, and closed his hand on the disc. When he opened his fingers again, the medallion was gone. 'Thank you,' he said again, and gave a great roar of laughter.

The Doctor grinned and unlocked the TARDIS door.

'Will they be all right?' Rose asked him as they stepped inside. 'Just the two of them?'

'Two? Three.' The Doctor turned in the doorway and gently ushered Rose back out again. 'I almost forgot. We should open the casket.'

'And that's another thing,' Rose said as the four of them gathered round the black coffin-like casket. 'Glint's out there somewhere. A murderous, homicidal, crazy pirate on the loose, ready to rob and pillage and… stuff.'

'I hardly think so,' the Doctor said. 'Open it.'

'Sure?' Rose said.

But before the Doctor could answer, Jimm had undone the clasp and swung the lid open.

They looked inside. And as the colour drained from her face and her legs went all wobbly, Rose realised the truth – what the Resurrection Casket was and what it did, and where Glint had gone. 'Oh,' she said. 'Blimey.'

McCavity's clothes lay in a muddled, empty heap. The baby in the casket looked up at them through large, deep blue eyes.

THIRTEEN

The mistake the idiots had made was to put her in a pod that did not rely on technology that would be affected by the zeg.

The Doctor had even told her as much, Salvo 7-50 thought with amusement. How space-crazy was that? Did he really think she would sail sweetly away from them and leave the Doctor and the others to escape unscathed after what they'd done to her shipmates – to her?

The Doctor was right, Salvo realised. There really was no choice in the matter. She ran her hands over the controls. The sensors in her metal fingers picked up readings of texture and composition, of temperature and surface detail. The dead human hand felt nothing at all.

The pod began to turn slowly on its axis as jets of compressed gas spat from the retro engines on one side. Through the cracked observation window, Salvo could see the pod containing the Doctor and his friends drifting slowly away. It would not take long to catch up, and when she did…

Her face broke into a half-smile.

Money of course was no object, so he secured the fastest steam yacht on Starfall. He knew where he was going and, although it had been many years since he'd crewed a ship, he settled immediately back into the familiar routine.

The steam yacht was soon making good speed towards Hamlek Glint's *Buccaneer*.

'Ah, what a sweet ickle baby. Did the nasty man become a little kiddie again, did he, didums?'

'Yes, thank you, Kevin,' the Doctor said. 'I think that's quite enough of that. Actually, I think rather than take Baby McCavity out you'd do better to close the lid again and fish him out when you get back to Starfall. Just as you did ten years ago.'

Rose was horrified. 'You can't shut the baby in a box!'

'It's that or a couple of days in an escape pod listening to his wailing, having nothing to feed him, and no spare nappies,' the Doctor said. 'Jimm's choice.'

'Let's close the lid,' Jimm said. 'He'll still be all right, won't he?'

'When you open the lid he'll be exactly the same as he is now. That's what happens. Living genetic material is extracted and projected. Then the old body is discarded and a new one cloned. That's what the Resurrection Casket does. That's what Kevin here and Bobb found out when they opened it the first time.'

Rose gaped. 'Bobb? You mean, Bobb…'

'Bobb is Robbie the cabin boy, yes. Or rather he was.'

'Getting a bit long in the tooth now,' Kevin admitted. 'But still the same old Robert Delvinny. They don't make 'em like him any more, I can tell you.'

'Uncle Bobb was a pirate cabin boy?' Jimm said. 'Oh, way cool! Why'd he never say?'

'I'm not sure he was actually all that proud of it,' the Doctor said. 'Though there was one thing he was proud of.'

Kevin nodded in agreement. 'The way he brought up Hamlek Glint, the way he nursed him as a baby and helped him grow into a boy. A boy he was determined would not follow in the same footsteps, a boy who would make a different choice about his life. Boy done good,' he said solemnly.

'Ten years ago,' the Doctor said, raising his eyebrows.

'But hang on,' Rose said. 'That would mean… Ah…' She laughed in nervous embarrassment. 'Right. Got it. Just call me Slow Rose, all right?'

Jimm stared at them, one after the other, his eyes wide as the porthole behind him. 'You don't mean…'

The Doctor slapped him on the shoulder. 'Sorry I blew up your ship,' he said. 'Cap'n. Ha-ha!'

Rose hugged Jimm. 'Don't worry,' she said. 'He's always doing that. Blew up my job when I first met him, then he took me to see my own sun blow up.'

'Oh, not fair,' the Doctor protested. 'That wasn't actually my fault, you know, it did it all by itself. Blew up your government, OK, fair enough. Though they were all aliens of course.' He broke off, realising that Kevin and Jimm were looking at him. Jimm was staring, open-mouthed. 'What? Look, never mind. Important thing is, you're making your choices, and I think Sad Sally's made hers. So, time we were going before the TARDIS packs up again.' The Doctor grinned as a thought occurred to him. 'Tell you what, p'raps I'll zeg-proof it and come back and see how you're doing one day.'

'That'd be good,' Jimm said. 'I…' He broke off and sighed. 'I don't know who I really am any more. What I should do.'

'Do you feel any different?' the Doctor asked.

'Well, no.'

'Then you're the same person as you always were. And you should carry on in just the same way, don't you think?'

Jimm shrugged. 'I suppose. It's a surprise but, yes, I guess it makes no difference.' He blew out a long, thoughtful breath. 'You need us to help push your box into the airlock?' he asked.

'No need, thanks,' Rose told him. 'We just sort of… go.'

'I can do that,' Kevin said modestly. 'In fact, I've a couple of things to sort out if you can spare me for a few minutes, Jimm. Be right back, though. Promise.' He turned to the Doctor and Rose. 'So, I'll say goodbye, then. It's been fun.'

'Hasn't it, though?' the Doctor said, grabbing Kevin's paw and shaking it enthusiastically.

'Oh yeah,' Rose agreed sarcastically. 'It's been a riot. Come here, big man.' She flung her arms round Kevin, and wasn't surprised to find they didn't reach anything like round him. She also realised, more than slightly embarrassed, that given his height she was probably clutching his buttocks. She let go quickly.

Kevin laughed, and hugged her back, almost squeezing the air from her lungs and cracking her ribs. 'Look after him,' he growled, nodding at the Doctor. 'I think he needs you.' Then to the Doctor, he said, 'Oh, and I'm sorry about... you know.'

'Oh, no problem,' the Doctor assured him. 'Happens. And good luck with seventeen across. It's a stinker.'

Kevin frowned, then the frown became a huge hairy smile. 'Bad Eggs. Of course. Thanks for that, Doc.' And in a puff of unsmoke, he was gone.

The Doctor laughed, and opened the TARDIS door.

'Bobb'll be surprised when we get back,' Jimm said.

The Doctor paused in the TARDIS doorway. 'Doubt it. I expect Kevin's nipped back a couple of times to tell him you're OK. He may not be pleased, but he won't be surprised. You take care of yourself. Make the right choices, yeah?'

'Yeah,' Rose told him. 'Have a great life. This time, do it right. You'll be fine. You'll be great.' She pulled Dugg's notebook from her jacket pocket and handed it to Jimm. 'Here you go – souvenir. His writing's terrible, but he scribbled notes on everything.'

'Like a logbook,' Jimm said. 'Thanks. It'll help me remember.'

'Captain's log, yeah. Remember our exciting time.'

'And the people who died,' the Doctor said. 'Remember Dugg. Remember who he was and what he did, won't you? Like Bobb remembers.'

'Yeah,' Rose told Jimm.

The boy nodded, his eyes glistening. Rose hugged him again, then followed the Doctor into the TARDIS.

'So Old Bobb planned to bring up Baby Glint the cut-throat pirate to be a respectable young man who never went into space?' Rose asked once they were inside.

The Doctor was busy at the controls. 'That's about it.'

'But will he grow up to be a murdering crazy pirate anyway?'

'With the start Bobb and Kevin have given him? I doubt it, but he always has that choice. After all, Bobb made a choice too, didn't he? On Jimm's behalf. He must have been surprised when he was presented with a newborn baby to bring up rather than releasing a terrifying, mature pirate. But he realised he could try to wean him off the life of blood and guts that Glint's previous incarnation plumped for. That's why Bobb's been so against Jimm hanging out with sailors. Well,' he added, 'there may be other reasons for that too, of course.'

'I bet.'

'And,' the Doctor said as the TARDIS engines ground into life, 'they do have Glint's treasure to see them through the rough times.'

'Yeah.' Then Rose realised what he'd just said. 'What?'

'That mock-up in Bobb's house. It's no more a work of art than McCavity's hideous death scene. It's the real thing. That's where the treasure's hidden – right where anyone can see it. I imagine Bobb discreetly sells off odd bits of it when he needs the cash. Which would be how the medallion got into McCavity's hands in the first place. Bobb just didn't realise what it was. Glint would've kept that a secret.'

'And what about Silver Sally?' Rose wondered.

The Doctor sighed and looked up from the controls. For a moment he stared sadly into the distance. 'Like I said, she's made her choice.'

Warning lights flashed in time with the klaxon. The whole pod was shaking as it tumbled out of control. At first, Salvo thought the Doctor had lied to her. But then she realised that was not the case. He'd misled her, made her think she could control the pod. But he had never lied.

And if she had stopped to think rather than acting out of blind, impulsive rage and the thirst for revenge, she'd have realised the pod must have some systems that would be affected by the zeg. That was, after all, why it was stuck here in the first place.

Life support was not something she'd needed until she sacrificed part of her metal soul to humanity. It never even occurred to her that it might fail and take the other systems with it. Now life support was killing her – that was a laugh.

Another explosion from somewhere deep in the pod's infrastructure. The ceiling was coming down, cables falling in loops and smoke billowing through. No way to control the engines now – no way to push herself out of the zeg. She just had to wait. She could feel the cabin pressure increasing as the atmosphere pumps went crazy.

Once the pod ruptured she'd be able to get out – then she could at least get to the edge of the zeg literally under her own steam. It would be a long wait. Parts of her would die from lack of oxygen, but the essential Salvo 7-50 would survive and wait and be rescued. One day.

There was a sound like breaking ice – a dry cracking. From the observation window. Soon it would break in half, shatter into pieces and let her out. But as she watched and waited, more of the ceiling collapsed.

A heavy metal stanchion struck her across the back, hammering Sally forward into the window and pinning her in position. She was spread-eagled across the cracking glass, staring out into the blackness.

'When it breaks,' she murmured to herself. 'When it breaks, I'll be out and free and safe.'

There was a polite cough from somewhere close by, just loud enough for Sally to hear. Then a gruff voice said, 'I really don't think that's true actually.'

She could turn just enough to make him out – the shaggy black shape of Glint's pet monster, sitting cross-legged on the floor close to her.

'Poll – er, Kevin!' she corrected herself. 'Thank goodness. You've come to save me.'

'Wrong again. I've come to check on you, not to help.'

'I don't need your help anyway,' she hissed. 'You pathetic pet parrot.'

Kevin nodded, as if this was what he'd expected. 'Have it your own way. You've got a lovely view, you know.' He stood up and walked over to join her, standing the other side of the heavy metal bar that held her firmly in place. 'The stars, the distant planets and moons, the wrecked ships in the zeg. Oh, and look – the graceful beauty of the waiting krarks.'

'What!' Salvo twisted back, pressing hard against the window. She felt it give, heard it crack again. And saw the streamlined shape of a krark emerging from behind a wrecked cargo liner and starting across the void towards her. Then another. And another.

'Anyway, you obviously don't need me. So, I'll just leave you to it, then,' Kevin said.

'No – wait. Kevin, my friend,' she pleaded. 'I always liked you.'

He sounded surprised and delighted. 'That a fact?'

'It was the others. Elvis and Cannon-K and the others, they were the ones who hated you, who made you do all those chores.'

'You don't say.'

'Help me, please. You can get me free, get the pod away from here and out of the zeg. Save me!'

Kevin folded his arms and leaned back against the glass. It bulged and creaked under his weight. 'I really can't help you,' he said. 'Sorry about that.'

The glass began to break. Hairline cracks webbed out from where Kevin was leaning, met and joined with other cracks. Kevin stepped back from the window. 'Oops,' he said. 'Actually,' he continued, his mouth close to Salvo's human ear, 'when I say I'm sorry I can't help you, that's not strictly true.'

For a moment she felt a glimmer of hope. 'You mean you *will* help me?' Just a glimmer. Just as the window exploded outwards.

'No. I mean I'm not sorry at all. Well, bye, then.'

Then the air in the pod was sucked out and she was floating suddenly free through the silent blackness.

The heavy metallic clang woke Jimm from his sleep.

He had been dreaming of pirates and adventure, of ships on fire and treasure lost and found. He blinked his tired eyes and turned quickly as the airlock systems hissed into life.

A suited figure was standing on the other side of the door, featureless helmet visible through the observation window. Jimm stared, holding his breath, wondering whether to hide. But he stood his ground. This was *his* ship – or rather pod – and no one was going to take it from him.

The hissing of air subsided as the pressure in the airlock reached normal. The figure at the window reached up and unclamped the helmet. Pale eyes stared in at Jimm, and the boy gasped in astonishment. He ran to open the door.

'Permission to come aboard, Captain,' the elderly man said.

He waited for Jimm to nod before stepping inside.

'You all right, lad?' Bobb asked.

'Yes,' Jimm said. His vision of Bobb was blurred. 'Yes,' he said again, though the word caught in his throat.

'Where's everyone else, then?' Bobb asked.

'Oh, Uncle Bobb, I've so much to tell you,' Jimm said. 'You used to tell me stories, and now I've got stories to tell you.' He held Bobb tight, struggling to reach round the bulky spacesuit.

'Reckon you have and all,' Bobb said, ruffling his adopted nephew's hair. 'Reckon you have.'

'Thanks,' Jimm said, but the word was almost lost in the hug.

'What for?'

'For coming to find me. For looking after me. For doing what's best.' Jimm let go and stepped back, looking proudly at his uncle. 'For everything.'

Bobb nodded. 'Least I could do,' he said. 'After everything you did for me.' And he pulled Jimm to him and hugged him again.

Unseen in the shadows behind the control console, something faded into existence. The hideous hairy monster watched his friends embrace and wiped a tear from his eye.

'Will Jimm manage?' Rose asked. 'Will he make it back to Starfall?'

The TARDIS quivered and spun and swam through the space between reality and non-existence, between time and emptiness.

At its heart, the Doctor fiddled with the controls and whistled a hornpipe. 'Manage?' he asked in a pause between verses. 'Of course he'll manage. He'll be magnificent. He has no choice about that.' He grinned. 'It's in his blood.'

Acknowledgements

As ever, I am indebted to a number of people, but in particular to both my editor, Stephen Cole – genius and gentleman – and Helen Raynor, script editor of the TV series, who gets to keep us all on course and up to scratch on all things *Who*.

About the Author

Justin Richards is the Creative Director for the BBC's range of *Doctor Who* books, and has written a fair few of them himself.

As well as writing for stage, screen and audio, he is the author of *The Invisible Detective* novels for children. He has a new series of children's books called *Time Runners* due in 2007, and his novel for older children, *The Death Collector*, was published in 2006.

Also available from BBC Books

DOCTOR · WHO

Monsters and Villains
By Justin Richards
ISBN 0 563 48632 5
UK £7.99 US $12.99/$15.99 CDN

For over forty years, the Doctor has battled against the most dangerous monsters and villains in the universe. This book brings together the best – or rather the worst – of his enemies.

Discover why the Daleks were so deadly; how the Yeti invaded London; the secret of the Loch Ness Monster; and how the Cybermen have survived. Learn who the Master was, and – above all – how the Doctor defeated them all.

Whether you read it on or behind the sofa, this book provides a wealth of information about the monsters and villains that have made *Doctor Who* the tremendous success it has been over the years, and the galactic phenomenon that it is today.

DOCTOR·WHO

The Stone Rose

By Jacqueline Rayner

ISBN 0 563 48643 0
UK £6.99 US $11.99/$14.99 CDN

Mickey is startled to find a statue of Rose in a museum – a statue that is 2,000 years old. The Doctor realises that this means the TARDIS will shortly take them to ancient Rome, but when it does, he and Rose soon have more on their minds than sculpture.

While the Doctor searches for a missing boy, Rose befriends a girl who claims to know the future – a girl whose predictions are surprisingly accurate. But then the Doctor stumbles on the hideous truth behind the statue of Rose – and Rose herself learns that you have to be very careful what you wish for…

The Feast of the Drowned

By Stephen Cole

ISBN 0 563 48644 9

UK £6.99 US $11.99/$14.99 CDN

When a naval cruiser sinks in mysterious circumstances in the North Sea, all aboard are lost. Rose is saddened to learn that the brother of her friend, Keisha, was among the dead. And yet he appears to them as a ghostly apparition, begging to be saved from the coming feast... the feast of the drowned.

As the dead crew haunt loved ones all over London, the Doctor and Rose are drawn into a chilling mystery. What sank the ship, and why? When the cruiser's wreckage was towed up the Thames, what sinister force came with it?

The river's dark waters are hiding an even darker secret, as preparations for the feast near their conclusion…